THE BESTSELLING SERIES
CONTINUES
WITH A BOLD NEW ADVENTURE!

"A continuously growing series of talented young SF authors . . . these books are really quite remarkable . . . the series promises to be well-received by Asimov fans."

—*Thrust*

"Like the movie serials of old, the publisher has me hooked, and I'll be watching the stands . . ."

—**Mark Sabljak,**
Milwaukee Journal

D1603474

ISAAC ASIMOV'S ROBOT CITY

ROBOTS AND ALIENS

Maverick by Bruce Bethke

A Byron Preiss Visual Publications, Inc. Book

ACE BOOKS, NEW YORK

This book is an Ace original edition, and has never been
previously published.

ISAAC ASIMOV'S ROBOT CITY
ROBOTS AND ALIENS
BOOK 5: MAVERICK

An Ace Book/published by arrangement with
Byron Preiss Visual Publications, Inc.

PRINTING HISTORY
Ace edition/August 1990

ISBN: 0-441-73131-7

Ace Books are published by The Berkley Publishing Group,
200 Madison Avenue, New York, New York 10016.
The name ''Ace'' and the ''A'' logo are trademarks belonging to
Charter Communications, Inc.

PRINTED IN THE UNITED STATES OF AMERICA

10 9 8 7 6 5 4 3 2 1

For John Sladek, Roderick,
and Clifford,
the world's stupidest springer spaniel.

INTRODUCTION

His memory has been erased. Hers was destroyed by a disease, and reconstructed with his help. His real name is David Avery, but he knows himself as Derec. Her name is Ariel Burgess.

Together they found Robot City and plumbed its mysteries. Derec, at peril to his life and in the throes of one of his mad father's experiments, learned to master Robot City and its robots. Hordes of chemfets—microscopic robots—in his blood gave him a direct connection with the central computer.

During a brief idyll, Derec and Ariel lived normal lives on Aurora. But Derec's final confrontation with his father had interrupted what the robots called the Migration Program—the program had not been canceled. Some robots had escaped from Robot City and had built new robot cities on new, uninhabited planets. Planets, at least, that were supposed to be uninhabited.

Supposed to be, but were not. Derec's placid interlude was shattered by a distress call from one of the new robot cities, telling of an attack. Rushing to the scene without Ariel, he and Mandelbrot discovered that the attackers were beings who looked something like wolves—a race of intelligent wolves.

First, there was a meteor flashing through the sky. Then the strange one came, the metallic-looking one they called

SilverSides, who never ate and wished only to protect the Kin and serve their wishes. It could only have been that SilverSides had been sent by the OldMother, ancestress and creator of the Kin. She had been sent to save them from the WalkingStones and the Hill of Stars they had built.

Not even SilverSides knows that she was a robot, cousin to the robots that were building a robot city on the Kin's planet. She had been designed and built not by Dr. Avery, Derec's father, but by Dr. Janet Anastasi, Derec's mother, who was running her own experiment in robotics.

SilverSides had been born shapeless, unformed, ready to imprint upon the first intelligent being she encountered. But the plan had not allowed for a robot city on the same planet. More intelligent than the Kin, SilverSides soon became their leader in the struggle against the robots. She launched a raid that crippled the city's main planning computer, and, recognizing Derec as the leader of the robots, attacked him.

Only Derec's invoking the First Law of Robotics saved him. But SilverSides was left with a dilemma. Were not the Kin human? How could they *and* Derec be human, and protected by the First Law? SilverSides took on the form of a human and the name Adam, but before this problem could be resolved there was another distress call—from Ariel. Joined now by Wolruf, Derec, Mandelbrot, and Adam went to her aid.

In Derec's absence, Ariel had gotten a call from yet another robot city. This one was also under attack by aliens, but aliens of a kind vastly different from the Kin.

Ariel found this robot city almost completely enclosed by a dome. This planet's inhabitants, the bird-like Ceremyons, were as advanced, compared to humans, as the Kin were primitive. Rather than attacking the city directly, they were sealing it under a dome where it could do no harm. The robots, following their programmed impulse to build and to prepare the planet for human habitation, were arranging to rebuild the city at a different location.

As soon as Ariel arrived, she summoned Derec through his internal connection with all the robot cities. But by the time he reached this planet, she had reached a tentative compromise—the Ceremyons, living almost all their lives in the air, would allow the robots to use some of the ground for farming, and they would allow one small enclosed city for the export of the food. Derec, with the help of the supervisor robots, reprogrammed the city.

Adam, still having no clear definition of what a human being is, imprinted on the Ceremyons, but they, needing no protection and having no need of his services, sent him back to Derec. Not yet certain to whom he owed Second Law obedience, he voluntarily set up his own agricultural experiment. In the course of this isolated work, he encountered a great silvery egg—an egg that he recognized as another being like himself, but not yet imprinted. Rushing back to the robot city, he brought Ariel to the egg in time for the new robot to imprint on her. Thus was Eve born.

Eve also went through the trauma of imprinting on the Ceremyons, but she encountered one who convinced her that he and he alone was human. Only his increasingly obvious insanity freed her from that dangerous illusion.

The agricultural reprogramming finished, Derec and Ariel and Wolruf decided to remove Adam and Eve from all possibly harmful influences—they would all go back to Robot City.

They returned to a Robot City in shambles. An unknown influence had seized control of the city's central computer, and tiny artificial humans—a few inches tall—were tucked away in many of the buildings. The robots had turned from maintaining the city to wild experimentation that reminded Derec and Ariel of the days of Lucius.

The obvious culprit was Dr. Avery. Although the experiments were of the sort that he had abhorred, he was the only one Derec knew who could seize control of the city. But while Avery did turn up in the city, he was so angry over the changes that he could not have been responsible. He was also no longer responsible for his own actions; he was now completely mad, convinced that he was turning into a robot.

Ariel took charge of the homunculi, and of Dr. Avery. She was more successful with Avery than with the tiny people, effecting the beginnings of a cure. Derec and Mandelbrot, meanwhile, tracked down the invading presence, an intelligence that called itself The Watchful Eye. This intelligence, it appeared, was guiding all the bizarre experiments in the hope of discovering the nature of human beings—and whether it might be one.

With the city collapsing around them, all forces joined to corner The Watchful Eye in its hidden lair. Finding it disguised as an ordinary piece of furniture, they at last forced it to reveal and face its true nature: the third of Dr. Anastasi's "learning machines."

Taking the name Lucius II, the new robot immediately entered an intense exchange of information with Adam and Eve. To the already unresolved question of what constitutes a human being, Lucius II added the possibility that these three robots may be humans.

These discussions took place in isolation from the humans and Wolruf. They were concerned with the issue of what to do with the packs of small, rodent-like animals that roamed the streets, a residue of some of Lucius II's experiments. Although they were clearly not human, these creatures had been generated using human genetic code as a starting point. Were they, then, also human, or could they be treated as vermin? This problem is complicated by Ariel's pregnancy, and the discovery that the fetus has been damaged by Derec's chemfets.

None of the medical robots on Robot City would even consider an abortion, since they considered the fetus human, even though it lacked a complete nervous system and could not survive birth. Adam offered to perform the operation in return for transportation back to the planet of the Ceremyons. The three learning machines hoped to consult with the Ceremyons on the question of humanity.

Robot City created a ship, which Dr. Avery named the *Wild Goose Chase*, from its own material. Surviving an accident that threatened all their lives, and Wolruf's definition as human, they reached the planet of the Ceremyons to discover that their elaborate plans had been canceled. Someone—a woman, and apparently a brilliant roboticist—had come and helped the Ceremyons reprogram the entire city. Derec and Dr. Avery tried to adapt the city to serve the Ceremyons, but at last the natives could find only one useful purpose for it. As the humans, Wolruf, and the robots left for the planet of the Kin, they saw the robot city slowly melting into itself, and taking on its new form as a vast metallic sculpture.

PROLOGUE
ARANIMAS

He sat before the horseshoe-shaped control console, like a hungry spider sitting in the middle of its web. Taut, alert, watching and waiting with an almost feral intensity; nearly immobile, except for his eyes.

The eyes: Two black, glittering beads set in bulging turrets of wrinkled skin on opposite sides of his large, hairless head. The eyes moved independently in quick, lizard-like jerks, darting across the massed video displays and instrument readouts, taking it all in.

Watching.

One eye locked in on the image of a small, starfish-like creature. His other eye tracked across and joined it as the video display split-screened to show the starfish on one side and the inky black of space on the other. A small ice asteroid drifted into view, and a pair of ominous-looking rails smoothly rose to track it.

He moved. An arm so gaunt and elongated, with carpal bones so long it gave the appearance of having two elbows, more unfolded than reached out to touch a small stud beneath the image of the starfish.

The grim, lipless mouth opened; the voice was high and reedy. "Denofah. Praxil mastica." The rails flared brightly.

An instant later the asteroid was gone, replaced by a swiftly dissipating cloud of incandescent gas.

The mouth twitched slightly at the corners, in an expression that may have been a grim smile. He pressed the stud again. "Rijat." The screen showing the starfish and the weapon went blank.

An indicator light at the far right end of the console began blinking. Swiveling one eye to the screen just above the indicator, he reached across and pressed another stud. The image that appeared was that of a younger member of his own species.

"Forrgive the intrrusion, Masterr," the young one said in heavily accented Galactic, with a piping trill on the "r" sounds. "But your orrders were to reporrt any K-band interferrence instantly."

Both eyes locked on the image, and he swiveled his chair around so that he was facing the viewscreen. "Did it match the patterrn? Were you able to get a dirrectional fix?"

"Master Aranimas, it *still* matches the patterrn. Rrobots using hyperspace keys to teleport; there must be *thousands* of them. We have both a directional fix and an estimated distance."

"Excellent! Give me the coordinates; I'll relay them to the navigator." While the young one was reading off the numbers, Aranimas swiveled his left eye onto another screen and pressed another stud. "Helm! Prepare for hyperspace jump in five hazodes." Another screen, another stud. "Navigator! Lay in the fastest course possible to take us to these coordinates." He repeated the numbers the young one had given him.

When the orders were all given and the screens all blank, he sat back in his chair, entwined his long, bony fingers, and allowed himself a thin smile. "Wolruf, you traitor, I have you now. And Derec, you meddlesome boy, I'll have your robots, your teleport keys, *and* your head in my trophy case." He reached forward and thumbed a button, and the starfish reappeared on a screen. "Deh feh opt spa, nexori. Derec."

The starfish seemed quite excited at the prospect.

CHAPTER 1
JANET

Attitude thrusters fired in short, tightly controlled bursts. With a delicate grace that belied its thirty-ton mass, the small, streamlined spacecraft executed a slow pirouette across the star-speckled void, flipping end-for-end and rolling ninety degrees to starboard. When the maneuver was complete, the attitude thrusters fired again, to leave the ship traveling stern-first along its orbital trajectory and upside-down relative to the surface of the small, blue-white planet.

Slowly, ponderously, the main planetary drives built up to full thrust. One minute later they shut down, and the hot white glare of the final deceleration burn faded to the deep bloody red of cooling durylium ion grids.

A final touch on the attitude jets, and the ship slipped quietly into geostationary orbit. Yet so skilled was the robot helmsman, so flawless the gravity compensation fields, that the ship's sole human occupant had not yet noticed any change in flight status.

The robot named Basalom, however, patched into the ship's communications system by hyperwave commlink, could not help but receive the news. He turned to the human known as Janet Anastasi, blinked his mylar plastic eyelids nervously, and allocated a hundred nanoseconds to resolving a small dilemma.

Like the really tough ones, the problem involved his conflicting duties under the Laws of Robotics. The Second Law

3

aspect of the situation was clear: *A robot must obey the orders given it by human beings, except where such orders would conflict with the First Law.* Dr. Anastasi had specifically ordered him to alert her the moment they entered orbit about Tau Puppis IV. He'd already cross-checked the navigator's star sightings against the reference library in the ship's computer; the small, Earthlike world currently situated some 35,000 kilometers overhead was definitely Tau Puppis IV. Unmistakably, his Second Law duty was to tell Dr. Anastasi that she had arrived at her destination.

As soon as Basalom started to load that statement into his speech buffer, though, a nagging First Law priority asserted itself. The First Law said: *A robot may not injure a human being, or through inaction allow a human being to come to harm.* Ever since they'd left the planet of the Ceremyons, any mention of the Learning Machine project seemed to cause Dr. Anastasi tremendous emotional distress. Even an implied reference to her son, her ex-husband, or the way the two of them had thoroughly bollixed the experiment by abducting Learning Machine #2 was enough to send the woman's blood pressure rocketing and turn her voiceprint into a harsh and jangled mass of severe stress indicators.

Now they'd returned to Tau Puppis IV, the world on which Dr. Anastasi had dropped Learning Machine #1. Basalom integrated that information with the data base he'd built up over two years of working with Dr. Anastasi, and concluded with 95% confidence that breaking the news to her would precipitate a negative emotional reaction. He could not predict exactly what her reaction would be—no robot was *that* sophisticated— but he could predict beyond a reasonable doubt that the information would cause Dr. Anastasi significant emotional discomfort.

And that was Basalom's dilemma. How did this emotional pain fit within the First Law definition of harm? His systems programming was not precise on that point. If emotional pain was not harm, there was little point to his being programmed to perceive it. But if evoking strong emotion was harm, then obeying Second Law orders could become a terribly ticklish business. How could he obey an order to tell Dr. Anastasi something that would upset her?

Basalom weighed positronic potentials. The order to provide the information had been emphatic and direct. The harm that would ensue—that *might* ensue—was only a possibility, and would, Basalom knew from experience, pass fairly quickly. In addition, he recalled from experience that Dr. Anastasi's reaction to his *not* providing the information would be just as extreme an emotion as if he *did* provide it.

The possibility of harming a human balanced; it was the same, no matter whether he acted or refrained from acting. He began downloading the statement to his speech buffer; as soon as he'd slowed his perception levels down to human realtime, he'd tell her.

Of course, if blood spurted out of her ears when he voiced the words, then he'd *know* that he'd caused some harm.

"Dr. Anastasi?" The slender blond woman looked up from her smartbook and speared Basalom with a glare. "We have entered geostationary orbit over the fourth planet in the Tau Puppis star system, mistress."

"Well, it's frosted well about *time.*" She reacted as if surprised by the tone of her own voice, rubbed the bags under her bloodshot eyes, and smiled apologetically. "I'm sorry, Basalom. I've shot the messenger again, haven't I?"

Basalom blinked nervously and did a quick scan of the room, but found no evidence of an injured messenger or a recently fired weapon. "Mistress?"

She dismissed his question with a wave of her hand. "An old expression; never mind. Is the scanning team ready?"

Through his internal commlink, Basalom consulted the rest of the crew. The reply came back as a dialogue box patched through to the scanning team, and a direct visual feed from a camera on the dorsal fin. From Basalom's point of view he saw Mistress Janet's image in the upper right corner and the scanning team's input/output stream in the upper left corner. Both windows overlaid a view of the ship's top hull gleaming brightly in the reflected planetlight, and as he watched, a long slit opened down the spine of the ship, and a thin stalk somewhat resembling an enormous dandelion began rising slowly toward the planet. At the tip of the stalk, delicate antennae were unfolding like whisker-thin flower petals and dew-sparkled spiderwebs.

"They have opened the pod bay doors," Basalom said, "and are erecting the sensor stalk now." He shot a commlink query at the scanning crew; in answer, data from the critical path file flashed up in the scanning team's dialogue box. "The stalk will be fully deployed in approximately five minutes and twenty-three seconds."

Dr. Anastasi made no immediate reply. To kill time while waiting for something further to report, Basalom began allocating every fifth nanosecond to building a simulation of how Dr. Anastasi saw the world. It had often puzzled him, how humans had managed to accomplish so much with only simple binocular vision and an almost complete inability to accept telesensory feeds. *How lonely it must feel to be locked into a local point of view!* he decided.

At last, Dr. Anastasi spoke. "Five minutes, huh?"

Basalom updated the estimate. "And fourteen seconds."

"Good." She leaned back in her chair, closed her eyes, and tried to work a kink out of her neck. "Boy, will I be glad to get this over with."

Basalom felt a tickle in his Second Law sense and formulated a suggestion. "Mistress? If there is another place you'd rather be, we can leave for it right now."

Dr. Anastasi opened her eyes and smiled wistfully at the robot; the expression did interesting things to the topography of her face. Basalom quickly scanned and mapped the wrinkles around her eyes, stored the image for later study, and then backed down to normal magnification.

"No, Basalom," Janet said, in that curiously slow output-only mode that humans used so often. "This *is* where I want to be. It's just . . ." Her voice tapered off into a little sigh.

Mistress Janet's last sentence didn't make immediate sense, so Basalom tried to parse it out. *It's just.* That broke out to *It is just.* Substituting for the pronoun, he came up with *Being in orbit around Tau Puppis IV is just.* Quickly sorting through and discarding all the adverbial meanings of just, he popped up a window full of adjective definitions. *Reasonable, proper, righteous, lawful,* see *Fair—*

Ah, that seemed to make sense. *Being in orbit around Tau*

Puppis IV is fair. Basalom felt a warm glow of satisfaction in his grammar module. Now if he only understood what Mistress Janet meant.

Janet sighed again and finished the sentence. "It's just, I've been thinking about old Stoneface again, that's all. Sometimes I swear that man is the albatross I'll be wearing around my neck the rest of my life."

Basalom started to ask Janet why she wanted to wear a terran avian with a three-meter wingspan around her neck, then thought better of it. "Stoneface, mistress?"

"Wendy. Doctor Wendell Avery. My ex-husband." Basalom ran a voiceprint across the bottom of his field of view and watched with familiar alarm as the hostility markers erupted like pimples in Dr. Anastasi's voice. "Derec's father. My chief competitor. The little tin god who's out to infest the galaxy with his little tin anthills."

"By which you mean the robot cities, mistress?"

Janet put an elbow on the table and rested her chin in the palm of her hand. "I mean exactly that, Basalom." She sighed, frowned, and went silent again.

Basalom stood quiet a moment, then switched to thermographic vision. As he'd expected, Dr. Anastasi's skin temperature was rising, and the major arteries in her neck were dilating. He recognized the pattern; she was building up to another angry outburst.

He was still trying to sort out the First Law implications of defusing her temper when it exploded.

"Dammit, Basalom, he's an architect, not a roboticist!" Janet slammed a wiry fist down on the table and sent her smartbook flying. "That's *my* nanotechnology he's using. My cellular robots; my heuristic programming. But do you think he ever once thought of sharing the credit?"

She kicked the leg of the table and let out a little sob. "The Learning Machine experiments were *beautiful*. Three innocent, unformed minds, experiencing the universe for the first time. Unit Two, especially; growing up with those brilliant, utterly alien Ceremyons. Just *think* of what we could have learned from it!

"But instead, old Stoneface dropped one of his architectural nightmares not ten kilometers away and ruined the whole frosted thing. Now Unit Two is traveling with Derec—Ghu knows *what* kind of hash is in its brain now—and the Ceremyons won't give us a second chance.'' Janet closed her eyes, plunked her elbows on the table, and put her face in her hands. ''I don't know what I did to deserve having that man in my life, but you'd think I'd have paid for that sin by now.'' Her voice fell silent; a little sound that may have been a sob slipped through her fingers.

Basalom watched and listened, the mass of chaotic potentials that symbolized uncertainty surging through his positronic brain. Mistress Janet was in some kind of pain; he understood that. And pain was equivalent to harm, that was also clear. But while the First Law kept demanding that he take some action to remove that pain, seven centuries of positronic evolution still hadn't resolved the question of how to comfort a crying woman.

He was saved from further confusion by a message from the scanning team that came in over his commlink accompanied by the video image of the sensor stalk at full extension. ''Mistress? The sensor pod is deployed and operational.''

She did not respond.

A minute later, an update followed. ''The scanning team reports contact with the transponder on the aeroshell, mistress. The flight recorder appears to be intact.'' Pause. More data flashed through Basalom's mind, and a tactical plot of the planet with projected and actual reentry curves popped up in his head. ''The pod made a soft landing within 200 meters of the planned landing site. Learning Machine #1 was discharged according to program. Preliminary imprinting had begun. All indicators were nominal.''

After a few seconds, Dr. Anastasi asked, ''And then?''

''The umbilical was severed, as programmed. There has been no further contact with Unit #1 since that time.''

Janet sat up, brushed back a few loose strands of her gray-blond hair, and dabbed at the corner of one eye with the cuff of her lab coat. ''Very good,'' she said at last. She pushed her chair back from the table and stood up. ''Very good indeed. Basalom, tell the scanning team to begin searching for the learning machine. Contact me the moment they find any sign of it.'' She began moving toward the door. "I'll be, uh, fresh-ening up.''

"Your orders have been relayed, mistress.''

At the door, she paused and softly said, "And thanks for listening, Basalom. You're a dear.'' She turned and darted out of the cabin.

Basalom felt the draining flow of grounded-out potentials that was the robotic equivalent of disappointment. Dr. Anastasi had called him a deer, but she'd left the cabin before he could ask her to explain his relationship to Terran herbivores of the genus *Cervidae*.

CHAPTER 2
THE HILL OF STARS

It was an old tradition, older than robotics itself. As was the case with so many of the behaviors passed down to robots from their human forebears, City Supervisor 3 found it to be slightly illogical; with the development of modern telecommunications technology, it had been several centuries since it was actually necessary for the participants in a conversation to meet physically. Yet traditions have a way of developing an inertia all their own, and so when City Supervisor 3—or as he was usually called, Beta—received the summons to an executive conference, he readily bowed to centuries of custom, delegated his current task to Building Engineer 42, and set out for the Compass Tower.

Not that it had been a terribly interesting task, anyway. He'd spent the last few weeks overseeing subtle changes in building designs, and the task he'd left was just one more round in a pattern of minor refinements. Beta's personality programming was not yet eccentric enough for him to admit to feeling bored, but ever since Master Derec had reprogrammed the robot city to cease expansion, he'd felt a certain sense of frustrated potentials. Installing a new and improved cornice simply didn't give him the same warm glow of satisfaction as came from, say, completing an entire block of luxury apartments.

Still, Beta reminded himself, *a job's a job. And any job that keeps robots out of the recycling bin is worthwhile.* Unbidden, a statement of the Third Law flashed through his mind: "A robot must protect its own existence, as long as such protection does not conflict with the First or Second Laws." *Yes,* Beta thought, *that's what we're doing. Protecting our existence. As long as we have jobs, we can justify our continued existence.* The Third Law potential resolved to a neat zero sum and stopped bothering him.

As he strolled toward the nearest tunnel stop, Beta allocated a few seconds to look around and review his earlier work. The avenue was broad, clean, and straight as a laser beam. The buildings were tall, angular, and functional, with no outrageous flights of engineering fantasy but enough variation in the use of geometric solids to keep the city from looking monotonous.

We certainly have fulfilled our original purpose. We have constructed a city that's clean, bright, and beautiful. One of the advantages of being a robot was that Beta could crane his neck and look up at the buildings without slowing his walking pace. *Perhaps we overdid it on the gleaming pale blue, though. Maybe next week we can paint a few things, just for contrast.* Looking down again, Beta found the entrance to the tunnel stop. He started down the ramp. Along the way, he passed a number of idle function robots.

For a moment he considered ordering them to report to the recycling bin. Then he felt a pang of—could it be *guilt?*—at the idea of destroying even non-positronic robots simply for the crime of being unemployed. Pausing a few microseconds, he managed to think up a busywork assignment for them. It was an illogical notion, of course, but he thought he detected a certain primitive kind of gratitude in the way they clanked off to their new jobs.

In a sense, we're all function robots. Some of us are a little more self-aware than others, that's all. Those function robots clean and lube things; I create gleaming, perfect buildings.

Why?

A dangerous question: Already, Beta could feel the stirring of a latent general command to self-destruct if he was no longer serving a useful purpose. Fortunately, with the summons to the executive council still fresh in his input register, he was able to duck that issue. He continued down the ramp.

A half-dozen idle tunnel transit platforms were waiting at the bottom of the ramp. Beta boarded the first one in the queue and gave it his destination. "Compass Tower." A fast scanning beam swept over him; the transit platform determined that its passenger was robotic and jumped into traffic with a neck-snapping jolt.

Always these subtle reminders, Beta thought. *The city was built for humans. Yet we who live here are not human.*

The platform shot through the tunnels at maximum speed, darting across lanes and dodging other platforms with reckless abandon. Beta locked his hands tightly on the grips and became a rigid part of the platform.

The force of air alone would knock a human off this platform despite the windscreen. Yet because I am a robot, the tunnel computer trades off safety for efficient traffic flow.

We built this city for humans. We are only caretakers.

So where are the humans?

An interesting question, indeed. And one that Beta could not answer.

With another rough jolt, the transit platform slid into the station beneath the Compass Tower and slammed to a stop. Beta unlocked his wrist and knee joints and stepped off; he only had one foot on solid pavement when the platform rocketed off into the storage queue. *As if there was a hurry.* Beta looked around the station, saw no one waiting to go anywhere, and dismissed the experience with the positronic equivalent of a shrug. Moving off the apron, he located the ascending slidewalk ramp and started up.

The meeting was to be held in the Central Hall. *An apt name*, Beta thought. *This pyramid we call the Compass Tower is the geographical center of the city. And Central Hall is at the heart of the pyramid.* That wasn't the real reason it was called that, of course; the name came from the fact that the hall housed Central, the enormous, disembodied positronic brain that ultimately controlled all activity in Robot City.

Or used to, anyway. Beta stepped off the last run of slidewalk and entered the cavernous hall.

He was immediately stopped by two hunter robots, tall and menacing in their matte-black armor. Tolerantly, Beta submitted to being surface-scanned, deep-radared, and bit-mapped. He was all too familiar with the need for tight security in this, the most critical of all places. After all, it was a lapse in security in this very room that had elevated him to the rank of Supervisor.

The hunters apparently were satisfied that he was who he claimed to be, and had legitimate reason for coming to Central Hall. They waved Beta through the checkpoint, and a moment later he stepped around the corner and got a good look at Central.

Even in its disabled state, Central was an impressive being. A collection of massive black slabs five meters high, resembling nothing so much as a silicon Stonehenge, it blazed with communication lasers, twinkled with monitor lights, and radiated an immense impression of great, dormant intellect on the 104-megahertz band.

At least, we hope it's intellect. A vague mismatch of positronic potentials flowed through Beta's brain; he identified the feeling as sadness. Pausing a moment, he watched the security observer robots drift overhead in tight, metric patterns, and stole sidelong glances at Positronic Specialists 1 through 5, who were once again up to their elbows in Central's brain.

Beta was capable of free-associating. Looking at the brain crew at work always reminded him of that terrible day—

Terrible? Beta caught himself. *A judgmental expression?*

Yes, Beta decided, *it was terrible.* Great responsibility had devolved on him that day a year before, when a malleable robot named SilverSides had appeared and adopted the wolf-like shape of the local dominant species. Breaking into Central Hall, it had attempted to destroy Central.

In that respect, SilverSides had failed. The backup and protective systems had kicked in in time to save Central's "life." The city had survived, and Central's authority was simply distributed to first-tier supervisors, like Beta.

In another respect, though, SilverSides had succeeded. Where once Central was a scintillating intellect that guided all the robots in the city and kept them working and thinking in harmony, now it was a babbling idiot-savant, full of bits and pieces of ideas, only occasionally lucid.

Still, we keep believing that it can be restored. We keep

telling ourselves that the damage caused by SilverSides can be repaired, and that it can again be the Central we once knew.

Is this another example of how we are evolving? Simple efficiency demands that we scrap Central and leave the supervisors permanently in charge. Yet we supervisors are reluctant to even suggest the idea. We keep insisting that our authority is only temporary, and that we will return power to Central just as soon as it passes diagnostics. That only Central is equipped to administer our fundamental programming.

Could that be the difference between being intelligent and being civilized? Valuing preservation of a fellow robot over efficiency? Caught between his evolving values and his orders to use resources efficiently, Beta felt himself drifting closer and closer to a Second Law crisis.

He was saved by the arrival of his fellow supervisors, Alpha and Gamma. Alpha spoke first. "Friend Beta, I have—with Central's permission—called this meeting to discuss the status of our mission."

Beta turned to greet the arriving robots. "Friend Alpha, Friend Gamma: I received your summons and I am here." Beta couldn't help but noting that his reply was a redundant statement of a self-evident fact; still the traditions had to be maintained. Alpha and Gamma walked past without breaking stride. Beta wheeled and joined them. Together, the three marched straight into the atrium at the heart of Central.

When they were in their assigned positions, Alpha raised his face and addressed the slab that held Central's console of audio/video inputs and outputs. "Central, we are here for the meeting."

"Hmmm?" Central's one great red eye glowed briefly, then dimmed.

"The meeting, Central. You remember, to discuss the status of our mission?"

"I have the greatest confidence in the mission," Central said.

"That's right, Central, we all have confidence in it." Beta and Gamma nodded, in support of Alpha. "And, now, if it's okay with you, we're going to discuss the status."

"What status?"

"Of the *mission*, Central."

"I have the greatest confidence in the mission," Central said, then he began softly singing "Daisy."

Alpha emitted a burst of white noise and turned to Beta and Gamma. "Let's get on with this. Beta, what exactly is our mission?"

Beta knew that Alpha and Gamma were both exactly as familiar with the mission as he was. After all, it was darned tough to forget something that was coded in ROM. Still, there were traditions that needed to be maintained, and the recitation of common knowledge was one of them.

"Robot City is a self-replicating mechanism designed to convert uninhabited planets for human use. Through the use of hyperspace teleportation keys and a unique, cellular robot technology—"

"That's enough, Beta." Alpha waved a hand to cut him off. "Gamma, what do you think is the most important word in our mission statement?"

Gamma's eyes glowed brightly. "The same word that's the crux of the Laws of Robotics. *Human*."

"Right." Alpha looked at Beta again, then back to Gamma. "We have successfully established a viable robotic community on this planet. We have initiated mining operations, developed a manufacturing base, and—insofar as Master Derec allowed— built a city. What's the one thing missing that prevents us from completing our mission plan?"

Beta thought of his clean, straight, empty streets, and his perfect, unused buildings.

"Humans," Central said. The heads of all three supervisors jerked up as if they were marionettes on strings.

"Central?" Alpha asked.

The great machine's one red eye glowed brightly. "French: *humain*. Latin: *humanus;* akin to humus, the ground. Pertaining to, belonging to, or having the qualities of mankind. 'The human species is composed of two distinct races, the men who borrow, and the men who lend.' Charles Lamb."

Alpha looked down again. "Forget it, Central."

"Forgetting." The red eye went out a moment and then came back on. "Oh, Alpha, you came to visit!"

"For—" Alpha caught himself. Turning to the other two

supervisors, he said, "So this is our problem. How do we serve humans if there are no humans here to serve?"

Gamma thought this over a moment. "There are humans on other planets, correct?"

"We can presume so."

"And they have some means of travel?"

"Again, we can presume so."

"Then we ca—ca—ca—"

Beta reached through to Gamma by commlink. *Priority override. Abort thought pattern.* Gamma's eyes dimmed, and he twitched inv̶o̶l̶ joint motors

̶ ̶ ̶ ̶ ̶ ̶ ̶ ̶ ̶ ̶ ̶ later. "Thank you, Beta. There's a strong ̶ ̶ ̶ ̶ ̶ ̶ ̶ ̶w block in my system. I can't even voice the thought.

Alpha nodded. "I know. I have the same block. Beta?"

"I also. However, if one were to phrase it carefully in passive voice, one could suggest that perhaps a robot with a quantity of hyperspace keys could be sent out to recruit human inhabitants."

Alpha agreed. "One could indeed suggest that. However, since we all share the common basic instruction block, one could presume that there are no robots in Robot City capable of carrying out this mission."

"In theory, I agree," Gamma said.

Alpha turned back to Beta. "So if one cannot recruit humans directly, and if one has a similar block regarding building a hyperwave transmitter and broadcasting our location, how would one go about finding humans to serve?"

"The indigenous species?" Gamma suggested.

Beta shook his head. "No. They are clearly not human."

"But Master Derec treated them as equals." All three supervisors fell silent.

In a small, hesitant voice, Central said, "A equals B."

Alpha looked up. "What did you say?"

"A equals B," Central repeated.

Alpha looked to Beta. "Do you have any idea what it's talking about?"

"If A equals B, and B equals C," Central said, quite confidently this time, "then A equals C."

Slowly, it dawned on Beta. "Central, is *A* human?"

"Yes."

"And is *B* Master Derec?"

"Yes."

Gamma broke in. "What's *C*, Central?" But the massive idiot had begun softly whistling an inane ditty.

Beta caught Gamma's attention. "Don't you see? If *human* equals Master Derec, and Master Derec treats the local inhabitants as *equals*—"

Gamma's eyes flared brightly. "Then the local inhabitants are equivalent to humans!"

Alpha protested. "Incorrect. A human is a primate of the genus *Homo*—"

Beta and Gamma both turned on Alpha. "We're not saying that the local inhabitants are truly human. We're just saying that they're *equivalent* to humans."

For long seconds, Alpha's eyes went dim. Just when Beta was beginning to worry about whether the supervisor had gone into First Law lockup, Alpha spoke.

"Agreed. For our purposes, we can treat them as near-humans. Now we have a new question: How can we best serve them?"

"That information is unavailable," Gamma said.

Beta considered the question. At the same time, not all of his energies were focused on the question; at a lower level in his brain, he sensed the joyous flow of harmonious potentials that came from finally having a clearly delineated problem to work on. "We must study the local environment," he said at last. "Send out observer robots to study the local inhabitants in their native habitat. Obtain chemical analyses of the substances that are important to their well-being."

"Agreed," Alpha and Gamma said together.

"Above all," Beta continued, "we must allocate all available resources to linguistic studies. We must establish verbal communications with them."

"Agreed."

Alpha stepped back and looked first to Beta and then to Gamma, with a warm glow in his eyes. "Friends, I cannot tell you how satisfied I am with the progress we have made in this meeting. Now, at last, we can fulfill the final goal of our mission.''

''I have the greatest confidence in the mission,'' Central said.

Alpha spit out a message at the maximum rate his commlink would allow. ''Meeting adjourned!'' Switching their leg motors into high speed mode, the three supervisors hurried from the hall as fast as dignity would allow.

CHAPTER 3

ARANIMAS

The assault team leader licked his lips nervously, as if punishment could be inflicted by hyperwave. "Yes, Master?"

Aranimas fixed the figure on the viewscreen with a glare from both eyes. "I am still waiting for your report. How many robots have you taken? Have you been able to capture the traitor Wolruf, or the human Derec?"

The assault team leader's right eye twitched rapidly, and he licked his lips again. "Actually, Master, we have encountered some, ah, difficulties, and, ah—"

Aranimas leaned in close to the video pickup, and dropped his voice to its most forceful pitch. "*How many robots have you taken?*"

With a fearful glance at his portable communicator, the team leader blurted it out. "None, Master."

"What?"

The team leader smiled helplessly. "We arrived too late. They're all gone. That static we intercepted was the sound of every last robot on the planet teleporting out. Apparently the natives—they call themselves Ceremyons—could not tolerate the robots. So the robots left."

Aranimas spat out several choice curses in his clan's dialect. When he'd recovered some control, he glared at the viewscreen again. "Did they leave any artifacts? Buildings, parts, or tools?"

"Sort of." The team leader turned his video pickup around to capture what he was seeing: a vast lake of liquid metal, crowned with two intersecting parabolic arches. The resolution was poor, but the arches appeared to be jets of silver liquid. "The natives say it's a work of art; they call it 'Negative Feedback.'" He turned the video pickup back on his face again.

Aranimas grumbled and rolled his eyes in counter-rotating circles. "One more chance, then. Have you located the traitor, or the humans?"

The team leader's expression brightened. "Yes, Master."

Aranimas waited a few seconds. When no further information was forthcoming, he said, "Where are they?"

"They left orbit three days ago and are headed in the general direction of Quadrant 224."

Aranimas grumbled again. "Not what I was hoping for. But very well, collect your team and return to the ship."

The team leader licked his lips once more and again blinked nervously. "Actually, Master, we have a little problem with that."

Aranimas' pale face flushed green with anger. "What *now?*"

"The natives are soaring creatures; they obtain lift by inflating their bodies with large amounts of raw hydrogen."

"So?"

"While attempting to extract information, I ordered the shuttle gunner to hit one of the natives with a low-wattage beam. I expected merely to burn the native; instead, it exploded with considerable violence."

"And the shuttle was damaged?"

"Not exactly, Master."

"*Not exactly?*"

"Master, the surviving natives have sealed the shuttle inside some kind of impenetrable force globe. It doesn't appear to be damaged, but we can't get to it. Could you send the second shuttle to extract us?"

Aranimas' heavy eyelids popped wide open, and his face turned a deep, angry green. "Bumbling fool! You can *rot* there for all the times you have failed me!" He slammed a bony fist down on the horseshoe console, blanking the team leader's face off his viewscreen. "Scanners! There is a ship in Quadrant 224; find it for me. Helm! Prepare to leave orbit immediately, maximum speed." Orders given, he blanked all the screens except one, and through that screen stared out at the glistening starfield in Quadrant 224. Somewhere out there, perhaps one of those tiny points of ninth-magnitude light, was the quarry he had been chasing for so long.

"I swear," he whispered, talking solely to himself, "I have not come this close only to be cheated again."

CHAPTER 4
DEREC

Ariel was in one of her cold and silent moods again. Derec tried to strike up a conversation over breakfast, but all he managed to do was irritate her more.

"Look, Ari," he said, "I know how you feel about losing the baby. I lost my whole *life*. When I woke up in that survival pod on the surface of that asteroid—"

A look of fury flashed into Ariel's eyes, and she fired a buttered scone straight at Derec's face. "Will you *shut up* about that stupid asteroid!"

He ducked the pastry and tried his most soothing voice. "But honey, my amnesia is—"

"Old news! You've been telling me about your frosted amnesia and that crummy little asteroid for the last three years. Don't you have any *other* stories?"

"Well, no, honey. The amnesia—"

"Aagh!" She threw another scone at Derec and this time caught him right between the eyes.

By the time Derec finished wiping the butter off his face, Ariel had locked herself in the bedroom. He briefly considered trying to reason with her through the closed door, and then realized that discretion was the better part of valor. Leaving her sulking in their stateroom, he decided to take a stroll around the upper deck of the good ship *Wild Goose Chase*.

The stroll went almost as badly as the breakfast. Within minutes Derec was thoroughly lost. As he wandered blindly through the great salons and companionways that simply hadn't been there the night before, the temptation to use his internal commlink to call for help grew very strong.

Derec resisted. *Frost*, he thought angrily, *for once I'm going to figure out this mouse-maze myself!* Pausing to visualize the latest floor plan of the deck, he thought once more about what a remarkable—and disturbing—ship it was.

Try as he might, Derec could not get used to the idea that he wasn't aboard a ship so much as he was *inside* an enormous robot. To make matters worse, the *Wild Goose Chase* was no ordinary robot, but rather one of his father's incredible cellular creations, constructed of the same amorphous robotic ''cells'' as Robot City itself. Back in Robot City, Derec had slowly come to accept that the city constantly rearranged its architecture to suit the perceived needs of its human inhabitants. But out here, in space—*far* out in space—there was something terribly unnerving about the idea of having nothing between himself and the vacuum except a ship's hull that changed shape like a Procyan jellyslug on a hot day.

For example, three days before, when they'd left the planet of the Ceremyons, the *Wild Goose Chase* had been reasonably ship-shaped: long, narrow, and linear, with the control cabin in the nose and the planetary drives in the stern. As soon as they'd cleared the atmosphere, though, the ship had decided to shorten the walking distance between the bridge and the engine room by reconfiguring itself into a thick, flattened disk not unlike an enormous flying three-layer cake. Derec had found being locked inside a Personal during that first transformation to be a terrifying experience. *Of course*, thought Derec, *it was for my own good. There was probably nothing but space on the other side of that door*.

Since then, the ship had continued to reconfigure itself in accordance with the expressed or implied needs of its passengers. Already a gymnasium, a synthe-sun deck, and a zero-G volleyball court had come and gone. These enormous, gaudily decorated new rooms puzzled Derec, though, until he remembered that he and Ariel had talked the night before about an old video she'd once seen. The show was some kind of ancient history swords-'n'-togas epic that took place on a steam-driven riverboat on Old Earth, and Ariel had been trying to make a point about the timeless nature of conflict in man/woman relationships.

But the ship, apparently, had picked up Ariel's appreciation for the sets and attempted to respond by recreating the promenade deck of an ancient Egyptian riverboat. No doubt by evening it would have dug enough Dixieland jazz out of its memory banks to provide music in the ballroom.

With a slight pang, Derec suddenly thought of three robots he'd once known. "The Three Cracked Cheeks would have loved this," he said sadly. "What a pity they're—" he caught himself— "*happily employed elsewhere and couldn't possibly be here*," he finished loudly. Already, he'd learned to be very careful about what he said out loud aboard the *Wild Goose Chase*. There was no telling what the ship might try to cook up to satisfy a perceived human need, and Derec had no desire to see it resurrecting cybernetic ghosts.

Just beyond the other side of the ballroom, Derec found a wide staircase that led down. It wasn't quite what he'd been looking for—he'd wanted to find a way to get up to the bridge—but curiosity led him to try the stairs.

The next level down was pure gray utilitarian metal. Even the environmental responses were down to a bare minimum: A puddle of light tracked him down the companionway, switching on two steps ahead of him and switching off two steps behind. The only door he found opened into a tiny, darkened cell.

His mother's three robots were in there. Adam, Eve, and Lucius II stood rigidly frozen in position, their eyes dim, as if someone had made an aluminum sculpture of a three-way conversation. For a moment, Derec's breath quickened. Ever since they'd left Robot City, his father had been itching for a chance to melt the learning machines down into slag, or at the very least shut them down permanently. Had he finally done it?

A quick check of his internal commlink, and Derec relaxed. The three robots weren't deactivated. They were simply locked up in one of their interminable high-bandwidth philosophical discussions. He moved on.

At the end of the hallway, he found a small lift-shaft much

like the one on the original asteroid where the robots had found him. It was a simple platform, one meter square, with one three-position switch on the control stalk: up, down, or stop. Obviously intended for robotic use—the sight of a human riding such a contraption would send most robots into First Law conniptions—the platform was also obviously at the top of its guide rail. "Well, that simplifies my choices," Derec said. He stepped onto the platform and pressed *down*.

With a sickening lurch, the platform dropped out from underneath him.

Derec didn't have time to panic. He fell through ten meters of darkness, then brightness flooded the shaft as the platform dropped through into a lighted cabin. Just before he passed through the opening, some kind of localized gravity field caught him and deposited him as gently as a feather, albeit sputtering like a goose, on the deck of the cabin.

Wolruf and Mandelbrot were already there, lounging comfortably in two acceleration couches that faced a large control console. The small, dog-like alien was spooning something that looked like Brussels sprouts in milk out of a bowl and between bites chatting with the patchwork robot. Her furry brown ears went up when Derec hit the floor; together, she and Mandelbrot turned to look at him.

" 'ullo," Wolruf said around a mouthful of greenery. "Nice of 'u to drop in."

Mandelbrot stared at Derec a moment, but did not rise. "Are you hurt?" he asked at last.

"Only my dignity," Derec said, as he got up off the floor and brushed some dust off his posterior.

"That is good," Mandelbrot noted. The robot turned back to Wolruf. "You were saying?"

" 'at can wait," Wolruf said. She favored Derec with a wicked grin, then barked out, "Ship! Master Derec wants t' sit next t' me!"

"That's all right, Wolruf, I can—*what!*" A glob of floor material suddenly mushroomed up under Derec, sweeping him off his feet and catching him like a giant hand. By the time it'd moved up next to Wolruf, it'd formed into another acceleration couch.

Wolruf leaned over, smiling wolfishly, and offered Derec a

dripping spoonful of whatever it was she was eating. " 'u want t' try some *gaach?* Is real good. Put 'air on 'ur face."

Derec looked at the thing on the spoon—which, on closer inspection, looked *nothing* like a Brussels sprout—and shook his head. "Thanks, I, uh, already ate."

Wolruf shrugged as if disappointed. " 'ur loss." With a practiced flip, she tossed the green globule up, then caught it with a frightening snap of her long teeth. "Mmm," she said in a deep, throaty growl that was apparently a sign of delight.

Derec finally recovered something of his composure, and started to look around the cabin he'd dropped into. "What . . . ? Why, this is the *bridge!*"

"T'row 'at boy a milkbone," Wolruf said between bites.

"But last night the bridge was at the *top* of the ship!"

Wolruf favored Derec with a toothy smile. " 'at's right. But 'at was 'en. 'is iss now." Derec kept darting nervous glances around the cabin, as if keeping an eye on everything would stop it from metamorphosing. Wolruf leaned over and put a furry hand on Derec's shoulder. "Face it, Derec. 'ur on a crazy ship." She shrugged.

"But iss not *dangerous* crazy." The little alien finished the last of her *gaach,* then licked the bowl clean with her long pink tongue. "Mmm," she growled again as she tossed the bowl and spoon over her shoulder, to clatter onto the deck.

"Wolruf!" Derec was shocked. "Do you always throw your dirty dishes on the floor?"

She rolled over, smiled innocently, and brought a hand up to start scratching her right ear. "What dishes?"

"Why—," Derec turned to point at it but stopped short. The spoon had already melted into the cabin deck, and only a tiny bit of the bowl's rim remained.

"Robot City maternal," Wolruf said with a shrug. "So 'ow's Arr'el?"

Derec watched the last trace of the bowl disappear, then sighed. "Still having a rough time."

"Th' baby?" Wolruf asked gently.

"Yeah." Derec fell back onto the couch and stared at his hands. "Ariel is still trying to pretend that she's too tough to mourn, I guess. So instead, she treats me like it's *my* fault she lost the baby.'' Derec fell silent a minute, thinking about the two-month-old fetus that Ariel had just lost. Maybe it *was* his fault. After all, the embryo's brain had been destroyed by an infestation of chemfets, the same microscopic robotic ''cells'' that swam in his bloodstream and gave him his incredible biological interface with Robot City. He should have realized that the chemfets were a communicable disease.

''Never 'ad pups myself,'' Wolruf broke in with a hint of sadness in her voice. ''But unnerstand that th' mother gets quite attached t' 'em long b'fore she actually whelps.''

''Yeah, well—look, this is depressing. Let's change the subject, okay? How's the flight going?''

'' 'u got 'ur depressors, I got mine.'' Wolruf sat up, and made a wide sweeping gesture that took in the control panel. ''Look a' it. Perfect automation. Don't need a pilot 'r navigator. I 'aven't touched a button in t'ree days, and probably won't until we jump tonight. No way I could everr fly 'er 'alf so good.'' Wolruf's upper lip curled in a silent snarl. '' 'ur father ever puts this design on the market, 'ur lookin' at one bitch 'oo's seriously out o' work.''

''That's okay,'' Derec said. ''We still love you anyway.'' To prove the point, he started giving her a reassuring scratch behind the ears.

''Oo! Oo! Don' stop!'' When her left foot began twitching reflexively, though, Wolruf got embarrassed and pulled away from Derec's hand.

Presently, a new thought came to Derec. ''Say, speaking of my father, have either of you seen him this morning?'' Wolruf shook her head, but Mandelbrot's eyes dimmed for a moment as he checked his internal links.

''Dr. Avery is in the ship's robotics lab,'' the patchwork robot announced.

''Robotics lab?'' Derec repeated.

''Yes. Dr. Avery had it constructed at 0137 hours last night. It is currently on the port side, two levels up.''

''Thanks, Mandelbrot.'' Derec bounced off his acceleration couch, said goodbye to Wolruf, then stepped over to the lift plate—and paused, to glare at the lift plate with obvious misgivings. ''Uh, ship?'' he said at last. ''I don't suppose you could cook up a *stairway*, could you?'' In response, a blank wall resolved into an arched passage that led to the bottom end of a spiral staircase. ''Thanks, ship.'' Derec stepped through the passage and started up.

Dusk came to the mountainside forest with the soft chittering of waking nightclimbers and the plaintive cooing of lovesick redwings. It came on a gentle southerly breeze that spoke of young green shoots bravely thrusting up through the warm, damp soil, and twisted old trees grudgingly coming to life again after yet another long dormant season.

Like the silent gray ghost of the winter just past, Maverick padded quietly through the lengthening shadows of the tall trees, alert to the soft sounds and drinking in the earthy smells of the warm spring evening.

He moved quickly and confidently across the needle-covered forest floor, as befitted an eighty-kilo carnivore with something on his mind. Yet there was a nervous twitch in his naked, whip-like tail that suggested different emotions at work; an occasional darting glance over his shoulder suggested he was not as brave as he seemed. At the edge of a clearing, as he stopped and stood up on his hind legs, it became apparent that he was favoring his left rear leg. For a moment the breeze ruffled his mottled grayish-brown fur, exposing the long pink scar of a recently healed wound; he was leaning against the tree trunk for support, not cover. Closing his ice-blue eyes, he lifted his muzzle and tasted the air.

A faint, acrid scent caught his attention. "Sharpfang!" He

added a guttural curse in BeastTongue; as if in answer, a deep bellow echoed across the valley.

Maverick's long, fur-covered ears shot up, and a look of puzzlement crossed his wolf-like face. "*That's* not right." He closed his eyes again, cocked his head sideways, and tried to concentrate on what the wind was telling him. "A female scent, but a male roar?" The bellow sounded again—quite nearby now—this time accompanied by the loud, rending crack of a fair-sized tree being knocked flat.

Maverick's eyes snapped wide open, and he grabbed for the stone knife in the scabbard on his left shoulder as if a knife could really be of use against a hungry sharpfang. A moment later the beast leaped into view not fifty trots away across the clearing, and Maverick froze.

The giant reptile charged across the clearing on its two massive hind legs, ploughing through the undergrowth and crushing everything in its way like a scaly brown juggernaut. Maverick stood rooted in one spot, staring at onrushing death. The sharpfang's head was huge; long, armored, and bristling with teeth, it whipped back and forth as if the beast had brain enough to feel fury. Long-taloned hind feet slashed through the brush; the thick, muscular tail trailing behind thrashed whatever had survived the talons into a pulpy green mass.

The sharpfang did not even break stride as it raised its head and opened its great jaws to roar again.

For a long fraction of a second, Maverick watched the dying sunlight flash off the beast's long wet fangs. Then he sniffed the air again, let out an anxious little whine, and dropped his ears in hope. Maybe, just maybe, the toothy monster wasn't interested in *him*. Allowing for windage, there was a family-minded female sharpfang down in the marsh about six hundred trots off to his left.

And if he were wrong?

Maverick carefully loosened the knife in its scabbard. With his injured leg, he knew he couldn't outrun the sharpfang. That left him only one other option: Wait until the beast was close enough to lick, and then hope that a fast and intelligent counterattack could overcome its overwhelming but mindless strength. He shifted his weight onto the balls of his feet. Reflexively, his naked, whip-like tail tucked itself between his legs and coiled around his thigh. He had to wait for the right moment; *exactly* the right moment. . . .

A moment later the advancing sharpfang apparently caught a whiff of the female and had a change of heart. It veered off toward the marsh. Saplings crunched; redwings screeched; Maverick stood his ground and pretended to be a tree stump. The beast passed close enough for him to take a long look straight into the fiery, bottomless red pit of its left eye.

Another moment later, and it was gone. Ears erect, Maverick listened to the crunching and roaring as it receded into the distance. Then he lolled out his long pink tongue, wuffed out a little laugh, and cracked into a wide, extremely relieved, panting grin. "They say love has no sense of smell. I'd guess it's blind, too."

He dropped to all fours, nosed around the base of the tree, marked it with his scent, and gave the male sharpfang more time to see if it was coming back for another pass or being followed by any competitors. When the forest at last grew quiet again, save for the thrashing and bellowing of giant lizards in love, he slipped the knife back into its scabbard and set off toward the northwest at a rapid trot.

"Well, Mavvy old boy," he told himself as he jogged along, "I'd say you handled that pretty well. There's not many kin who'd stand up to a charging sharpfang like that.

"Of course, the old ones always said that it's the running away that attracts their attention."

He paused to sniff around the base of a rock outcropping and mark it with his scent. Then he went on.

"But here's another thought: Their eyes are on opposite sides of their heads. Maybe the reason sharpfangs swing their heads when they walk is because they can't see what's straight in front of them.

"Interesting idea, Mavvy. So the best way to attack a sharp-fang is from right under its chin? That little piece of information ought to be worth something to the next pack we run into." At the thought of a pack, his left rear leg gave him a little twinge to remind him of the last pack he'd run into. "Ooh. A bad night for rock climbing, old boy. Still, it's got to be done."

After a year as a packless outcast, Maverick had stopped

noticing that his silent thoughts had turned into one-kin conversations.

He detoured around a patch of stingwort, stopped to mark another tree, and then continued. "But while we're on the subject of sharpfangs: Mother, they sure are noisy things, aren't they? It's a wonder they ever manage to surprise a hunting pack.

"Actually, no it isn't. The kin in hunting packs spend so much time arguing with each other and bickering over status, the wonder is that *they* are ever able to surprise anything."

As the last ebb of the sunlight slipped away, Maverick finally broke out of the tall forest and reached the foothills. He sat down, paused for a reflective scratch, and stared up at the forbidding, rocky crags.

"Yes," he told himself, "running solo is definitely the way to go. No status fights, no orders, no drooling little pups slowing you down."

His voice took a darker turn. "No food, no warm cave to sleep in, no family." Maverick's voice dropped to a breathy whisper, as if he had finally become aware that he was talking to himself. "Let's face it, lad. We've been on the run too long. We—*I* have got to find a pack to join." He thought back on the winter he'd just lived through and shuddered involuntarily. "I've got to find a pack *soon*." Taking a deep breath, he dug his paws into the loose gravel and started up the side of the mountain. Smallface, the lesser of the two moons, was just rising. He had a lot of climbing to do before Largeface rose.

Halfway up the slope, he surprised a feeding whistlepig. The stupid little furball tried to hide in plain sight; scrabbling and clawing, Maverick fell on it and bit its head off with one snap of his long, toothy jaws. The meat was tough and nearly tasteless, but he carefully chewed and swallowed each bite.

Excluding carrion, it was the first meal he'd eaten in three days.

Robotic Law potentials danced and capered in Basalom's positronic brain like fireflies on hyperdrive. Impulses and reactions chased each other through his circuits, laughing riotously as molecular relays burst open and slammed shut like hallway doors in an old comedy routine. As much as a robot can be said to enjoy anything, Basalom was beginning to *enjoy* the incredibly complex nets of conflicting potentials that wove themselves inside his brain. Now, with the latest news just in from the scanning team, an entirely new dimension was added to his decision matrix, imparting a wonderful sense of energy to his cognition circuits. The potentials glittered in his mind like an Auroran filterbug's web on a dewy morning.

Dr. Anastasi was *not* going to like the scanning team's report.

First and Second Law conflicts skirmished in his brain, fighting for priority. Each time his decision gate flip-flopped, the stress register escalated. When the register hit 256, the accumulated potential was shunted to ground through his optical perceptor membrane actuator.

In simpler terms, he blinked.

Dr. Anastasi finished her business in the Personal and emerged into the companionway. Basalom blinked once more to clear his stress register and then addressed his mistress.

"Dr. Anastasi? The scanning team reports finding no trace of Learning Machine #1."

"*What?*"

Again, a surging clash of potentials! How could he obey the implied Second Law command to repeat and clarify the message without violating the First Law by insulting her intelligence?

Basalom settled for slowing his voice clock rate by ten percent and augmenting his speech with "warm" harmonics in the two-kilohertz range. "For the past eight hours, the scanning team has worked outward in an expanding radial pattern from the landing site. Within the limits of their equipment, they have not been able to find any evidence of Learning Machine #1's existence."

Dr. Anastasi ran a hand through her hair. "That's impossible. It was powered by a cold microfusion cell. Even if the learning machine was completely destroyed, they still should be able to pick up residual neutron radiation from the power pack." Then a thought crossed her mind, and she frowned. "Unless Derec . . ."

She shook her head. "No, a coincidence like that would strain credulity. The scanning crew must have made some mistake." She turned and started up the companionway toward the bow of the ship. "Well? Come along, Basalom."

Basalom was almost disappointed. His lovely, complex decision matrix resolved to simple Second Law obedience, and he dutifully fell in behind.

To minimize the effect of stray radiation from the ship's engines on delicate equipment, the scanning team's cabin was located in a blister on the underside of the uttermost bow of the ship. To get to the blister, Basalom and Dr. Anastasi had to leave the cargo bay laboratory, walk the entire length of the living quarters, and then drop down one level to the low-ceilinged companionway that ran beneath the bridge. For the last ten meters, they had to pull themselves along handholds through a narrow, zero-gravity access tube.

Along the way, to keep his mind busy, Basalom reopened his human viewpoint simulation file. He had more observations to add to the file and more data to correlate. In particular, Basalom wanted to record an effect that he had noticed twice before: That Dr. Janet, when given information she did not like, would insist on traveling to the source and verifying the information herself.

This must be a corollary effect of having a purely local viewpoint, Basalom decided. *Dr. Anastasi would rather believe that a severe failure has occurred in her information gathering systems than accept unpleasant information.*

Basalom logged, indexed, and stored the observation. *Someday I will meet robots who have been observing other humans in a similar fashion. Perhaps then we will be able to integrate our data and formulate fundamental laws of human behavior.*

Perhaps someday, Basalom repeated. But given the way Dr. Anastasi shunned human society, it was not likely to be any time soon.

Puffing with exertion and the indignity of it all, Dr. Anastasi pushed off the last handhold in the access tube and floated into the scanning blister. A moment later Basalom followed; he immediately noted that the four robots that made up the scanning team were still jacked into their consoles. He fired off a quick commburst suggesting that they turn around and look sharp. Slowly, awkwardly, the four robots began disconnecting their umbilical cables, detaching themselves from their consoles, and switching over to their local senses.

Looking at the squat, blocky machines, Basalom felt a surge of the positronic flux that he identified as a feeling of superiority. The scanning team robots were plain metallic automatons designed expressly for work in zero-G. They had ungainly, boxlike bodies, no heads to speak of, and in place of proper arms and legs, eight multi-jointed limbs that ended in simple metal claws. Since the bulk of their sensory data was routed through the scanning consoles, they came equipped with the bare minimum of human-interface hardware: one audio input/output membrane and a pair of monochrome optics on stalks. The effect, Basalom decided, resembled nothing so much as a quartet of giant softshell crabs.

Strike that. Basalom ran a quick cross-reference through his metaphor library. *Make that, they look like giant lice.*

Dr. Anastasi was still waiting patiently for the scanning team to finish disconnecting themselves, so Basalom allocated a few microseconds for comparative analysis. *They are crude, func-*

tional devices. I have a humanoid configuration, human-like limbs, and an acceptably human face.

They are little more than human-friendly front-ends for the machines that they are connected to. I am intelligent, perceptive, and equipped with refined sensibilities.

Verily, I am molded in the image of my Maker!

Then a new, unknown potential surged through Basalom's circuits, and he reevaluated the results of his analysis.

Still, they are my positronic brothers, and I must help them elevate themselves if I can.

Basalom didn't realize it, but he had just become the first robot in history to be condescending.

The last of the scanning robots finished disconnecting itself from its instrument console. As one, the four robots rotated their sensory turrets to "face" Dr. Anastasi.

When she was sure she had their attention, Janet began issuing commands. "Eyes, Ears, Nose, and Throat! Report!" As soon as that last word left her lips, Basalom anticipated the cacophony that would result from a literal interpretation of that order and jumped in on the commlink. *Override,* he squirted out to the scanning robots. *Report sequentially.*

The scanning robots seemed to accept his authority. Eyes, the robot in charge of scanning in the infrared through ultraviolet portion of the spectrum, began reporting first in a flat, toneless voice.

"Using the design information available for Learning Machine #1, I projected its range of possible operational profiles and thermal dispersion patterns. I found no infrared sources in the target area which met this criteria.

"Next, I used the solar spectrographic information and atmospheric data supplied by Nose, along with our knowledge of Learning Machine #1's physical structure, to compute the albedo—"

Basalom interrupted via hyperwave. *Explain albedo.*

"—That is, the optical wavelength reflectivity of its skin. Allowing a 15-percent variance for self-directed changes in surface texture, I still was unable to identify any objects which showed a high probability of being either part or all of the learning machine.

"Finally, based on the knowledge that the 'cells' that compose the learning machine are actually polyhedrons with microplanar surfaces, I scanned for moiré patterns in the ultraviolet range. Aside from the aeroshell in which the learning machine landed, I found nothing to match my search profile.''

Good job, Eyes. The squat little robot did not acknowledge Basalom's compliment.

Dr. Anastasi nodded thoughtfully. "I see. Next?"

Ears, the robot in charge of monitoring the microwave through hyperwave portion of the spectrum, began reporting in an identical monotonous voice. "While I have been able to locate the transponder on the aeroshell, I have not received any signals from Learning Machine #1's built-in hyperwave transponder. Nor have I been able to detect any leakage of the kind that should be associated with the operation of the learning machine."

Dr. Anastasi's brow wrinkled.

Explain leakage, Basalom hyperwaved.

. "When operating, all cybernetic circuits emit a certain amount of electromagnetic radiation. If we are familiar with the design of the device, we can project the frequency and data encryption of the leakage. No leakage conforming to the learning machine's profile was found."

Dr. Anastasi nodded. "I understand."

"Learning Machine #1 was equipped with an internal commlink," Ears went on. "I have been monitoring the base channel that you assigned to it, but I have been unable to pick up any signals originating from Learning Machine #1."

Dr. Anastasi frowned. "Okay, I hear what you're saying. Next?"

Nose, the robot in charge of spectrography and chemical analysis, spoke up. It was equipped with the same voice synthesizer as Eyes and Ears, but Basalom noted that a microscopic crack in Nose's voice diaphragm gave it an interesting third-harmonic distortion.

"My specialties are of limited use in this situation. However, I was able to coordinate with the other units. I provided Eyes with spectrographic data regarding the Tau Puppis sunlight and a summary analysis of the planetary atmosphere. Beyond that, I am unable to contribute."

Dr. Anastasi frowned. "Hmm. Something smells fishy about that. I'll have to think it over. Next?"

Throat, the robot in charge of outbound telecommunications, spoke last. "Due to our inability to locate the learning machine, laser and maser communications were not attempted. I have been broadcasting continuous messages on the learning machine's internal commlink frequency. However, as Ears reported, there has been no response."

Dr. Anastasi shot Throat a cold stare. "You don't say?"

That was a rhetorical question, Basalom added. *Do not answer.* The robot held its silence.

Dr. Anastasi looked the scanning crew over one more time and screwed her face up into a look of complete disgust. "I can't believe this," she said finally. "You robots have been scanning that ball of dirt for eight hours and you haven't found *anything?*"

Throat did not wait for a cue from Basalom, but simply spoke right up. "On the contrary, Dr. Anastasi, we have found a great deal. However, none of it matches the profile of either the learning machine or its damaged remains."

Dr. Anastasi forgot about Newton's laws for a moment and waved a hand to cut Throat off. Unfortunately, since she was floating in zero-G, the action sent her spinning toward the neutrino detector. Basalom gently caught her and stabilized her.

"You found something? *What?*"

Eyes answered the question. "I have detected a significant number of large lifeforms in the area of the landing site. The largest appears to be a warm-blooded grazing animal. The next largest appears to be a cold-blooded predator which follows the grazing animals as they migrate. Since we do not know the final shape of the learning machine, I can tell you only that the average predator outweighs the learning machine by a factor of four to one."

Dr. Anastasi frowned. "Oh, great. So our learning machine ran into a monster and got itself demolished."

The scanning robots conferred briefly by commlink. "It is possible," Throat said. "However, in that case we would still expect to find identifiable wreckage. At the very least, we should be able to locate the microfusion cell. We have not found either.''

"Moreover," Eyes continued seamlessly, "I have detected a number of clustered infrared sources. The sources are almost always found in the vicinity of what appear to be limestone caves, and the next largest class of lifeforms are generally found clustered around the infrared sources.''

Dr. Anastasi looked from one robotic "face" to the next with a very puzzled look in her eyes.

Basalom squirted out a hyperwave message to the scanning team. *Clarify!*

"I studied the spectrographic signatures of the infrared sources," Nose said. "I detected cellulose, chlorophyll, carbon, and pyroligneous acid.''

"So our intelligent lupoids are still down there. But they couldn't have destroyed the learning machine, and they sure couldn't have removed all traces of it.

"If the robot were inside a cave, would you be able to detect it?''

Eyes, Ears, Nose, and Throat conferred briefly. Ears spoke when they had finished. "The commlink would penetrate all but the deepest caves. Small amounts of positronic leakage from the brain should also be detectable. I detected neither.''

"So something is rotten in the state of Denmark," Dr. Anastasi said.

Basalom was still trying to parse out the metaphor when Janet kicked off the wall and dove into the access tube. "Let's get out of here. I need time to think.''

As he followed, Basalom reopened his human viewpoint file and made another entry. *When Dr. Anastasi wants to avoid having to make a decision, she moves to a different part of the ship and claims a need to think. Does physical location have a significant effect on human cogitative abilities?* He logged and indexed the entry; as he was storing it, a dialogue box popped open in the upper left corner of his field of view.

Basalom? It was Eyes. *This reaction puzzles us. Have we harmed Mistress Janet by giving her this information?*

Basalom responded via commlink. *I am still trying to determine the First Law implications of emotional distress.*

Oh. Eyes was not a particularly bright robot, but it was self-

aware enough to realize that it lacked experience in the subtleties of dealing with humans. *In that case, perhaps you are
best qualified to judge whether or not we should report our
one additional finding.*

I will try. What is it?

There was a pause; nothing a human would have noticed,
but Basalom could plainly see that the scanning robot was
having difficulty integrating the information. *While we were
unable to locate the specific communications and energy signatures of Learning Machine #1, we did record a significant
amount of other robotic activity.*

Basalom's curiosity bits skyrocketed. *Other robotic activity?
Explain.*

The little robot made one more try at generating a conclusion
from its data and then gave up. *I cannot. Stand by for download
of raw data.*

Basalom cleared several of his unused memory banks, re-
directed his I/O to fast storage, and opened his multiplex comm
channel. *Ready.* A nanosecond later, a torrent of raw data
flooded into Basalom's mind. As fast as he could, he sorted,
collated, and organized the data. Pushing it through his pattern-
recognition algorithm, he tried to isolate and identify the most
important points.

One by one, the points swam into clear focus. They quickly
formed a structure, a simple pattern that teased comparative
memories out of his long-term data storage.

Oh no. His stress register started clicking like a geiger
counter, and the pattern took on an ever-more-familiar shape.
It can't be. His First Law sense began to itch like mad as the
Second Law potential tried to find a route to ground. One word
got out through the First Law filter: "Madam?"

Dr. Anastasi paused in the tube and looked over her shoulder
at Basalom. "Yes?"

Power flowed through Basalom's cognitive circuits like
strong wine. Thoughts spun and danced; potentials crashed and
exploded like thunderclouds on a hot summer night.

"Madam, there—" The First Law choked him off again.

A concerned look crossed Dr. Anastasi's face. "Well?"

In Basalom's mind, the First and Second Law collided head

on, drew apart, and collided again. Neither was the clear win-
ner; he sought desperately to reroute data to his speech centers.

"Ma—"

Dr. Anastasi grew impatient. "Come on, Basalom. Spit it
out."

His limbs froze; his major joints locked up. He blinked sixty-
four times in rapid succession, and then through sheer force
of will dumped his speech buffer through his voice synthesizer.

"There is a Robot City on this planet."

CHAPTER 7
MAVERICK

The spur of rock jutted straight out from the side of the mountain forming a natural balcony. Maverick sat on the edge of the spur, drinking in the clean pine smell of the forested valley below and watching the moons' light glitter and dance on the river in the distance. Smallface was now near its zenith, and it cast a cool, white light with almost no shadow. Largeface, just barely above the horizon, was a dull orange globe the color and shape of a vingfruit with a bite taken out of it.

Somehow, the sight of the two moons together in the sky stirred something deep and primal in Maverick's soul. As if the two were directly linked, his excitement grew as Largeface rose. He paced nervously around the rock spur. A half-dozen times he yelped sharply when he thought he heard something. His excitement only grew stronger when the sounds turned out to be false alarms.

Then the sound he'd been waiting for came wafting gently on the wind, and it was raw, beautiful, and absolutely unmistakable.

At first, it was very soft and distant. *Arooo*. Just one voice at first, lonely, plaintive, and far away. The sound sent chills up and down Maverick's spine and set his hackles standing on end.

Then another voice joined in, a little closer. *Arooooo!* The first voice responded, and the forests and mountains threw back the echo of the ancient, wordless cry.

No, those weren't echoes, those were yet more voices, joining in the chorus of a song that was as old as his race. Voices joined, and picked up, and repeated. *AROOO!* The call carried for miles across the hills and valleys. Not just miles; hundreds of miles, as the voices followed the rising moon west across the land. As it had on certain nights for thousands of years, the song chased the twin moons clear across the world, from the eastern shores to the western sea.

When he judged the time to be right, Maverick threw his head back, flattened his ears, and joined in. *AROOOO! I am Maverick! I am here, my brothers! I join you! AROOOOOO!*

Other intelligible words began rising out of the joyous, incoherent howl of BeastTongue. *I am ChippedFang.*

I am DoesNotFollow.

I am RaggedEar.

I am SmellsBad. I join you!

The Howl Network had just come on line.

The Howl Network reached from sea to sea, and from the land of AlwaysSnow to the Uncrossable Desert. It covered the land, but it was not terribly efficient. Maverick had plenty of time to think while listening to the threads of news that twisted through the air.

This time, though, he thought silently. *How strange, lad. The pack-kin insult and despise the outcasts. If they catch you in their territory—and outnumber you by at least three to one— they'll attack you, and even try to kill you.*

Yet if it weren't for the outcasts, not a one of them would ever know what was happening just fifty trots outside his pack's territory.

Oops. A message that he found interesting echoed through the night. Maverick picked it up, repeated it, and added a few comments of his own. Then he went back to thinking.

Hmm. I add comments, and ChippedFang adds comments, and DoesNotFollow adds comments. . . . Might be interesting sometime to get the originator and the final receiver of the message together, to see how much the message changes along the line.

More messages wafted through the damp spring air. Weather reports from out west; looked like heavy rain this year. Further accounts of renewed fighting between two feuding packs in the southeast; oh, those two had been fighting for years without resolution. A hunting report on the grazer migration in the north; it seemed the calves were fat and slow this year, and the sharpfangs few in number. Maverick dutifully picked up and repeated each message without comment, then went back to his first line of thought. •

Yes, the pack-kin hate loners. They attack you; they warn their pups that they'll turn out like you if they aren't good. They call you pups of the FirstBeast, and blame you for everything that's wrong with their cozy little world.

Maverick thought of the last pack he'd encountered, less than a week before. The freshly healed scar on his leg gave him another sharp twinge, but he smiled anyway, and for a moment lost himself in a memory of soft young fur and a certain long pink tongue.

Yes, the pack-kin hate you. But on warm spring evenings when the mood is in the air, their virgin daughters seek you out.

And when their huntleaders are all dead or driven off by internal fighting, who do they ask to be their new leaders?

Maverick stood up on all fours a moment, yawned as wide as his jaw would allow, and indulged in a long stretch that ran from his haunches clear out to the toes of his forepaws. Then he treated himself to one more smile.

''Face it, kid. They're just plain jealous.''

Oops! A new message was coming through the night, and he'd almost missed it. Maverick quickly sat down, cocked his ears, and listened attentively to the voice—he thought it was RaggedEar—that relayed the story.

''—report from the eastern lakes country. The kin of PackHome are seeing GodBeings again.

''PackHome was the scene of last year's so-called 'Hill of Stars' incident, in which an enormous, shining sanddigger's nest reportedly appeared in the midst of isolated hunting territory.

''The sudden appearance of the Hill of Stars was accompanied by an invasion of 'WalkingStones.' These creatures, which walked on their hind legs at all times and had no smell, killed several kin by throwing lightning from their fingertips.

"At about the same time, a mysterious kin known as SilverSides joined the pack. She destroyed several of the WalkingStones, and forced the GodBeing that lived in the Hill of Stars to come out for single combat. Local kin say that SilverSides became a GodBeing herself and went into the Hill of Stars.

"Since then, SilverSides has been seen only once, in the company of a strange, half-kin, half-GodBeing creature named Wolruf."

Wolruf? Maverick wondered. *What's a wolruf?*

"LifeCrier, who speaks the history for the kin of PackHome, says that SilverSides was a gift of the OldMother and has returned to her. LifeCrier insists that SilverSides will return to lead the hunt and protect all the kin.

"Young kin from many packs have come to the eastern lakes country to hear LifeCrier speak and hoping to glimpse the GodBeings. But there are stories of widespread confusion.

"In the meantime, the faithful wait, and the Hill of Stars itself remains silent. This report was first cried by StormBringer on the eastern lakes echo."

Maverick sat quietly a few moments longer, listening to the last reverberations of the message die out against the mountainside. Then the yips and howls started up again as other kin picked up the story and repeated it. Maverick cleared his throat, laid his ears back, took a deep breath—

And thought better of it. "PackHome, eh? In the eastern lakes country?" He squeezed out a tight-lipped smile, got to his feet, and trotted over to where the spur of rock joined the side of the mountain. "Sounds like a chaotic, leaderless mess to me." At the top of the trail he paused to look at the stars and get a good fix on the direction he was heading. Then he started carefully picking his way down the talus-covered slope.

"Just the place for a strong kin with a little ambition, eh, lad?"

He looked up at the stars one more time and noted that

LargeFace was now well up in the sky. In this phase the shadowy outline of SplitEar, the kin in the moon, stood out very clearly.

Maverick couldn't help but feel that old SplitEar, first pup of the OldMother, was smiling down on him.

Dr. Avery was hunched over a data terminal in the ship's robotics lab, deeply engrossed in a dense mass of hex code, when Derec called out, "Hi, Dad!" and came bouncing into the room.

Avery pulled his face away from the terminal just long enough to glare at Derec. "Will you please stop calling me that?" he asked, his white mustache bristling with anger. "You know how much it annoys me."

"Sure, Dad."

Avery shot his son one more if-looks-could-kill glance, ran his fingers through his long white hair, and turned back to the terminal. He would never have said it out loud, of course, but in his heart, Avery admitted that Derec certainly had every right to try to annoy him. After all, it was Avery's megalomaniacal experiment that had erased Derec's memory and infected Ariel with amnemonic plague. Now he could not reconstruct how, in his madness, he had caused the amnesia, much less how to reverse it. And while his little chemfet nanomachines had ultimately worked to perfection, they'd nearly killed Derec twice, and they *had* killed Derec and Ariel's unborn child.

Given all that, Avery resolved once more to put up with whatever juvenile revenge Derec was in the mood to exact today. He waited patiently while Derec found a noisy tin stool, dragged it over, and sat down. Then, when it appeared that Derec wasn't going to say anything, he called up another bloc of code.

"Whatcha doing, Dad?" Derec asked brightly.

Avery sighed and turned to his son. "I'm going through the ship's systems software, in hopes of finding the shape-changing algorithm."

"Why?"

"I'd like to stop the polymorphism, or at least slow it down a great deal."

"Why?"

Avery sighed again and ran his fingers through his hair. *That's one of the problems with having children raised by robots*, he thought. *When they're about three years old, they go through a "Why, daddy?" stage. The Second Law forces the robots to answer. So the kids never outgrow it.*

Avery straightened his lab coat, pasted on his best imitation paternal smile, and answered the question with another question.

"Have you ever walked off the edge of a gravity field?"

Derec sifted through his attenuated memories. "I don't think so. Why?"

"I did, last night. You've seen how minimal the environment on the second deck is? I was looking for Lucius last night and I walked into a pitch-dark cabin that had no gravity field."

"What happened?"

"When you reach the edge of a gravity field, you don't float up into the air. Rather, *down* suddenly becomes the floor of the room you just left. There's no sensation of falling; you simply pivot on the doorsill and follow the field through a 90-degree curve."

"So?"

"Have you ever heard the expression, 'the floor jumped up and hit me in the face'?"

Derec snickered.

"Blast it, Derec, it's not funny! If the floor hadn't realized what was going on and softened itself an instant before impact, I would have broken my nose!"

Derec tried to keep the laugh suppressed, but a small giggle found a crack and wiggled through.

Avery scowled at Derec through his bushy white eyebrows. "You think that's funny? This morning I happened to think out loud that I needed to use the Personal, and frost me if the chair I was sitting on didn't transform itself into a toilet!" Avery shot a savage glare at the ceiling of the cabin. "And no, I do *not* need to use the Personal now!" His chair, which had begun to soften around the edges, quickly firmed up again.

Derec sputtered twice and then exploded into uncontrolled laughter.

Avery's scowl melted. "Okay, maybe it's a *little* funny. But I'll tell you, the thing that finally pushed me over the edge was the nightmare I had about one this morning. I dreamed that the ship had transformed itself into a giant humanoid robot and was insisting that its name was 'Optimus Prime.'"

Derec abruptly stopped laughing, and his face went pale. "Gad, that's a horrible thought."

"Woke *me* up in a cold sweat, I can tell you."

After a few seconds of thoughtful silence, Avery turned back to his workstation and slapped a hand on the data display. "Anyway, that's when I decided that the shape-changing program had to go. Or at least, it had to get toned down some." He looked at Derec, attempted a tentative smile, and then looked around the robotics lab.

"You know, son, there are some really good ideas here. Take this ship's skin, for instance; cellular robotics is the perfect technology for seamless, self-sealing spacecraft hulls. If we could just find some way to bond the robotic skin permanently to a titanium-aluminide frame, we might really be on to something." He turned to Derec and cautiously met his eyes.

"Derec? When we get back to Robot City, we're going to have to work on this design some more."

Derec nodded and looked away. He never enjoyed admitting it, but every once in a great while his father could be right.

While Derec's face was turned, Avery stole a few moments to really *look* at his son. It was funny, but despite the nearly twenty years that had passed since Derec was born, Avery couldn't remember ever once just looking at the boy and seeing him for what he was. He'd always looked at the boy and seen what he wanted him to *become*. For most of the boy's life, Avery now noted with a little sadness, he'd treated Derec more like an experiment than a son.

Derec. Even that name was part of an experiment. The boy's real name was David, but Avery had wiped out that memory along with everything else. This young man who stood before him now, fidgeting uncomfortably and staring at the wall— this *Derec*—was a stranger.

But blood will tell. While Derec looked away, Avery studied the line of his jaw and the shape of his cheekbones. He saw his ex-wife Janet's genes everywhere; from the sandy blond hair, through the pale complexion, to his thin, expressive lips.

And what did I give you, my son? Avery didn't need to ask; he knew he'd given Derec the traits that didn't show. *I gave you my temper, I'm sorry to say. I gave you my coldness, and my fear of being vulnerable*. Not for the first time, Avery felt a sudden need to hug his son.

The moment passed. *I'm sorry, Derec. I can't open up either*. Still, that didn't mean he couldn't build just a little bridge, did it? Avery decided to take a chance.

"So what do you think, Derec? Would you like to give me a hand? The ship can cough up another robotics terminal in a couple of minutes, and I could use the help."

Well, son? Please?

Derec said nothing, but his face turned tight and thoughtful. Avery watched closely; Derec's body language said that he was trying to say yes. The word was working its way up to his lips, but it was a fight every inch of the way. It had started in his gut, clawed its way up his esophagus, and traversed his soft palate. It was on his tongue now; at any moment it would break through to his lips. Derec started to open his mouth—

The intercom buzzed. It was Wolruf.

"Derec? We got somethin' 'ere. 'u better come 'ave a look at it."

Derec broke concentration, swallowed hard, and turned to the intercom panel. "Can it wait? I'm a little tied up at the moment."

Wolruf growled something in her native tongue. "Think 'u better come look at this *now*."

"Oh, okay." Derec turned to his father, cracked a weak

smile, and shrugged. "Sorry, I have to, you know." He gestured toward the intercom and left the sentence hanging.

"That's okay. We can continue this another time." Avery offered Derec a smile.

Derec just looked at his feet and shrugged again. "Sure. If you want." Another hesitation, and then he turned and darted through a pair of open lift doors that had appeared in the cabin wall.

The lift doors hissed open, and Derec stepped out onto the bridge. Mandelbrot stood in one corner, staring intently at the external visual display and conversing with a data terminal. Wolruf was crouched over the main control console, her thick, sausage-like fingers flying over the controls like a multisynth player performing Mothersbaugh's "Toccata and Fugue in .25 Kilohertz." As she punched keys and adjusted sliders, she kept up a steady stream of short, guttural commands in both broken English and her native language. The console seemed to be accepting both with equal ease.

The lift doors slid shut. Derec cleared his throat and said, "Okay, Wolruf. Where's all the excitement?"

Wolruf neither turned around nor took her hands off the controls. Instead, she simply lifted her head a little and pointed her nose at the visual display. " 'ere."

Derec looked at the display. It was the view astern, he guessed; the exceptionally bright star off to the right side looked about the right color to be the Ceremyon's sun. Aside from that star, though, he saw nothing that appeared out of place on the usual visiplate starfield.

"So? I don't see anything."

Wolruf growled something untranslatable and started pounding on a different section of the control console. "Sorry. Keep forgettin' 'u 'umans eyes are almos' as weak as 'ur nose." The visual display shifted, blurred, and came into focus again.

More starfield. Only this time there was a tiny, smudgy gray blob in the middle of the screen.

"Okay, I see it now," Derec said. "What is it?" He moved to stand next to Wolruf, but the blob wasn't any more meaningful when viewed close-up.

Wolruf glared at the little blob and bared her teeth. "Ast'roid," she said with a growl.

Derec looked at her. "All this fuss over an asteroid?"

"This 'uns been gainin' on us for eight hours."

"What!" Derec spun around and looked at the visual display. The blob still wasn't any more meaningful than it was before.

Wolruf punched in a few more commands, and the display went back to its original image. This time, though, a graceful blue curve was superimposed over the starfield. "Allowing f'r mass, and all known gravitational vectors includin' th' cavitation effect of 'ur drives, here's th' projected orbit for th' ast'roid." She punched two more keys, and a jagged red line twined around the blue.

"And 'ere's its actual course."

Cautiously, Derec touched the visiplate. He traced the red line with a finger, stopping on one particularly sharp bend. "Any known phenomena that could cause this?"

Wolruf shook her head.

" 'At bend 'u got 'ur finger on iss a manual course correction I made ten minutes ago." Wolruf continued. "Five minutes later, the ast'roid changed course to match."

Wolruf paused to lay her ears back and look Derec straight in the eye.

"Derec, 'at ast'roid iss under *power*."

Derec studied the visual display a bit more and then looked back to Wolruf. "Recommended action?"

Wolruf gritted her teeth and crouched low over the controls. "Recommend we find out 'oo's behind it. Also recommend 'u find 'urself a seat. 'iss could get a littl' *rough*." She shot a fierce grin at Mandelbrot, then slapped a finger down on the intercom button. "Arr'el? Dr. Av'ry? 'old on tight, we're makin' an unprogrammed course correction. *Now*."

An acceleration couch popped up out of the cabin deck; Derec just barely had time to dive into it before Wolruf slammed the ship into a violent roll. The starfield in the viewplate spun dizzily.

The ship was still rolling when Wolruf hit the main thrusters.

In all, the experience wasn't as jarring as Derec had expected. The ship's gravity fields did an exceptionally good job of compensating for the changing gravity and thrust vectors.

Unfortunately, they didn't do a thing for Coriolis force. Within instants, Derec was feeling thoroughly dizzy and a little nauseated. He wondered how Ariel was taking it.

Then he wondered about something else; about a story he'd once read. "Wait a minute, Wolruf. This won't work."

Wolruf cocked an ear at Derec, but kept flying.

"It can't work. The angles of incidence are all wrong. If someone's behind that asteroid, all he has to do is use his maneuvering thrusters to keep the rock between him and us. The asteroid's too small for us to enter a gravitational orbit; at this range, there's no other way we can fly around it faster than he can maneuver around it."

Wolruf kept flying. Mandelbrot, back in the corner, spoke up. "Mistress Wolruf has already thought of that. I have all ship's sensors locked on the asteroid. If the unknown vessel emits any form of radiation or hot gasses during maneuvering, we will detect it."

"'sides," Wolruf growled, "'aven't 'u ever 'eard of spookin' 'im out? If 'e's got some kind of remote sensor watching us, 'e now knows we know 'e's there. No point in 'im staying 'idden any more."

As if in confirmation of Wolruf's statement, Mandelbrot said, "Contact. A stream of superheated boron-11 has just been emitted by a source behind the asteroid."

Wolruf's mouth opened in a toothy grin, and her tongue lolled out. "We *got* 'im." She fired a last round of maneuvering thrusters and stabilized the ship's course. "Now let's see—"

"More contacts," Mandelbrot said. "Additional thruster exhaust; I am projecting—

"Cancel. Visual contact. I am putting it on the main viewer." The stars swam, blurred again, and resolved into a much closer look at the asteroid than Derec had had before.

A ship was creeping out from behind the right edge of the asteroid. At first glance it looked like a fairly conventional Settler design. Then Derec realized that he was just looking at the foremost piece of it.

The ship came out from behind the asteroid, and kept coming. It wasn't just large, it was *enormous*. And yet the design had a curiously improvised look about it, as if someone had decided to build a supervessel by simply welding together a dozen randomly selected hulls. Sleek trans-atmospheric hulls nestled in with ungainly cargo pods, and a hodgepodge of angular bracing and spaghetti-like tubing connected the whole lot. Bits of it looked like standard Spacer equipment, or Auroran pleasure yachts, while other segments looked utterly alien, like nothing Derec had ever seen before.

Then he felt the touch of an icy ghost finger on his shoulder, and the hairs on the nape of his neck stood straight up. He *had* seen a ship like that before.

Derec glanced quickly at Wolruf. Her hackles were standing up, and she'd bared her teeth. Derec suddenly knew he didn't need to ask what she was thinking.

"The approaching vessel has opened fire," Mandelbrot announced. "Primary armament appears to be phased microwave lasers."

As one, Derec and Wolruf looked at each other. *"Aranimas!"*

Wolruf became a flurry of action. She slammed her fists down on controls, jabbed buttons, and barked terse, almost hysterical commands at the ship. In response, the ship yawed hard and pitched wildly as the main drives erupted into life.

"This is impossible," Derec said. "We destroyed Aranimas in Sol system. I *saw* his ship explode."

"'u saw 'im jettison second'ry 'ulls." Wolruf punched up some kind of intersecting curve display, peered at it anxiously, and resumed hitting controls. "On my world there's a small liz'rd called a *skerk*. 'u grab its tail, th' tail breaks off. Skerk gets away, 'u get its tail." She glanced up at the screen again; the flying junkyard was still closing. "'u must 'ave got a piece of Aranimas's tail."

Derec just stared at the viewscreen and shook his head. "But how in the universe did he find us again?"

"Don't know," Wolruf growled. "Matter of fact, don't care. Just know we need to get away *now*." She leaned back to survey the control board settings and then thumbed the intercom button. "Arr'el! Dr. Av'ry! Stand by for jump!"

"Jump?" Derec shouted. "We can't jump! We're too far away from the programmed jump point."

"Direct hit on the stern," Mandelbrot announced.

"Wolruf! You didn't have time to calculate and enter a new course!"

Wolruf punched more buttons. " 'u care about details at a time like thiss?"

"Another hit," Mandelbrot said. "Hull breached in Section 17D."

"But where will we go?" Derec wailed.

"Someplace Aranimas *issn't!*" Wolruf took one last glance at the control settings, and then grabbed the jump control handle and yanked it down hard.

A shift, a spin, Derec felt a rolling disorientation in his inner ear: Enormous energies were expended, and the *Wild Goose Chase* squeezed through a hole in the space/time continuum. A moment later, it was somewhere else.

Wolruf engaged the autopilot. With careful and precise thruster bursts, the ship stabilized its tumble. The viewscreen blanked, cleared, and displayed a binary star consisting of a yellow giant and its white dwarf companion.

With obvious effort, Wolruf relaxed her grip on the jump handle and sagged back into the acceleration couch.

"Where are we?" Derec asked softly.

Mandelbrot spoke up. "I am working on that. We will have a rough navigational fix within six hours, and coordinates precise enough to begin programming another jump in twenty-three."

"Twenty-three hours? But what if Aranimas follows us?"

"Then we are caught." Mandelbrot exchanged a stream of bits with the data terminal. "Given the availability of free hydrogen in this system, it will be a minimum of ninety-one point five hours before we have accumulated enough hydrogen to fuel another hyperspace jump."

Derec frowned. "Well, if that's it, then, it'll have to do. Deploy the ramscoops, Mandelbrot."

"I have already done so."

"Thanks. Wolruf?"

The small alien rolled over and looked at Derec with eyes that had gone past fright and were now simply exhausted.

"Wolruf? You were his navigator once. How did Aranimas find us again?"

Wolruf brought a foot up and scratched her ear thoughtfully. "Don't know."

"But his sensor technology—"

"Iss whatev'r 'e can steal. No tellin' what 'e's got now.'"

Derec frowned again. Then his face brightened. "Well, there's no point in worrying about it. As Mandelbrot pointed out, if he can follow us, the *Goose* is cooked." He turned to Wolruf and smiled. "But I don't think that's a real issue. We got away clean. I mean, every schoolboy knows that it's physically impossible to track a ship through hyperspace, right?"

Wolruf got up on one elbow, reached across the couch, and rested a furry hand on Derec's shoulder.

"Derec," she whispered, "I don't think Aranimas went to 'ur school."

CHAPTER 9

WHITETAIL

Old LifeCrier, spiritual leader of the kin of PackHome and self-proclaimed First Believer in SilverSides, sat at the mouth of the cave, watching the milling throng in the clearing below. "Do you hear that, daughter?" he said proudly, using the informal words of KinSpeech. "They're all speaking my name."

From somewhere inside the cave, WhiteTail answered, "That's sweet, Father."

He ignored the humoring tone in her voice and looked back out over the crowd. "'LifeCrier,' that's what they're saying. 'We've traveled for days to hear LifeCrier.'" He let his tongue loll out and smiled clear back to his fourth bicuspids. "You never thought your old father would be heard beyond the pack."

WhiteTail carried a few old dry bones up from the darkness and deposited them in the rubbish heap near the opening. "Of course I did, Father." She turned to head back into the darkness, but he reached out a paw and gently stopped her.

"Look at them, WhiteTail. Just *look* at them. What do you see?"

WhiteTail stood up on her hind legs and surveyed the crowd. Then, with a disgusted snort, she dropped back down to all fours. "I see about two hundred extra mouths to feed. We're running low on food as it is."

The old kin smiled sadly and shook his head. "Oh, ye of little vision. That's the beginnings of the Great Pack out there."

WhiteTail sniffed disdainfully. "It's a hungry mob of outcasts, younglings, and losers, that's what it is. Not ten decent hunters in the lot of them. And certainly no hunt leader."

LifeCrier ignored her. "*Think* of it, daughter. We have the privilege to be a part of the greatest thing that's ever happened to the kin. First SilverSides came down from the OldMother. Now the Great Pack is forming. Soon all the packs will be united, and the sharpfangs will be driven away forever. We're seeing untold generations of prophecy fulfilled right before our very eyes!"

WhiteTail sighed heavily and cast a distempered look at her father. "Do the prophecies say anything at all about how we're supposed to feed them?"

"Oh, my short-sighted daughter." He tried to wrap his tail around her shoulder, but she shrugged it off. "Still thinking about mere physical needs when we have the spiritual sustenance of SilverSides?"

WhiteTail jumped to her feet and impatiently twitched her long, whip-like tail. "All I'm saying is that somebody better do some hunting around here, or SilverSides is going to be short a few followers if she comes again."

"*When,* daughter." LifeCrier slowly roused to his feet and stretched out in an easy yawn. "*When* SilverSides comes again, she will lead us to all we could ever hope for. Good knives. Warm furs. More food than, than—"

WhiteTail's eyes narrowed. "Yes? I'm listening."

"Well, more food than you can imagine, anyway. We won't want for anything."

"And in the meantime we're just supposed to sit and wait patiently?"

"Don't worry, daughter. SilverSides will lead and protect us. She promised she would. Just as she promised that she would return."

WhiteTail turned around in a tight, nervous circle, glared at her father, and turned around again. Whatever was left of her patience finally gave up the ghost.

"You addled old fool! For twelve days and nights now you've kept the hunt here in PackHome and filled their heads with stories of SilverSides! In the meantime, the bellies of the younglings growl with hunger and the pups are crying because their mothers have no milk!''

LifeCrier turned to face her; involuntarily, WhiteTail's hackles went up and her lips drew back in a snarl, exposing double rows of needle-sharp teeth.

''Father, I don't *care* if SilverSides is coming back someday. Your pack is starving now! You call yourself the leader of PackHome; when will you get your head out of the sky and lead the hunt?''

LifeCrier sagged back on his haunches and let his ears fall flat. With a sudden start, WhiteTail noticed the pain and confusion in the old kin's eyes. ''My own daughter,'' LifeCrier whispered. ''My own daughter challenges me.''

Seeing the pain in her father's eyes, WhiteTail felt a sudden stab of remorse. Fighting for control over her emotions, she lowered her hackles, crouched down on her belly, and laid her head on her forepaws. ''I'm sorry, Father.'' She looked up at him with big, sad, puppy-dog eyes. ''I spoke without thinking. I said things I didn't mean.''

LifeCrier stood up, trotted over, and gave her a friendly little nuzzle behind the ears, as he used to when she was just a pup. ''That's all right, WhiteTail. Every now and then the FirstBeast gets into all of us and makes us say things we didn't mean.'' She relaxed, and gave him an apologetic lick on the muzzle. LifeCrier returned a paternal smile. ''I'm sure SilverSides forgives you for your momentary lapse of faith.''

With great effort, WhiteTail kept her hackles down.

LifeCrier gave her one more nuzzle behind the ears, and then started poking around in the sleeping furs that lay piled in one corner of the cave. ''Now, where did I leave that amulet? Ah, here it is.'' LifeCrier pulled out the badge of his office—a broken circuit board suspended from a braided necklace made of robotic nerve wire—and slipped it over his head. ''Well, it's time to address the faithful. Coming, Daughter?''

At first she was going to demur, but then the germ of an idea occurred to her. Suppressing a wicked smile, she sweetly said, ''Of course, Father. I'd love to be with you.'' The old kin got to his feet and trotted out of the cave with WhiteTail beside him.

The barking and yipping started the moment someone in the crowd spotted LifeCrier. A few in the crowd gave themselves up to their excitement and howled in BeastTongue. By the time the old kin had crossed to the rocky knoll that overlooked the clearing, the noise had resolved into a rhythmic chant: "*Life*-Crier, *Life*-Crier, *Life*-Crier . . ."

WhiteTail stopped at the base of the knoll and watched her father as he climbed. At the top he paused a moment to look out upon the crowd with a broad, tail-wagging smile on his face. All eyes were on him, he knew, and he basked in the glory. Then he sat down, flattened his ears, closed his eyes, and raised his voice in a long, mournful howl of BeastTongue.

The crowd returned his benediction. The sight and sound astonished WhiteTail; over two hundred kin all packed into a clearing, sitting with their backs arched stiffly, muzzles raised in a deafening unison howl.

LifeCrier dropped his head and switched to the formal cadences of HuntTongue. "Listen!" Abruptly, the howling stopped. "Hear me, O kin! I tell of the time before time, and of a promise made to our mother's mother's earliest dam."

"Praise the OldMother!" an excitable convert near WhiteTail shouted. She looked him over quickly and found him much like the others: scruffy, underfed, possibly good-looking if he'd just groom his fur. But there was a little too much hunger in his eyes, and he sported a fresh scar on his left rear leg. *Another loser,* she decided, dismissing him with a sniff.

"Listen!" LifeCrier said again. "In the beginning, there was the Great Pack. They lived in the Forest of Dawn, when the world was young. Of game there was no end; of enemies, none that dared invade the dens of the kin. Each hunter had his perfect mate, each little mother her strong and obedient pups, and all the kin lived in harmony. All the days were green and cool, and all the nights were warm and sweet, for time had not yet begun and Death was a stranger to the kin. It was forever summer in the Forest of Dawn, and great were the blessings that the OldMother showered down upon the kin."

"Praise the OldMother!" the convert shouted again, this time getting the cue right.

LifeCrier's face darkened, and his voice took on an ominous

tone. "But though they were blessed, those first kin knew it not. Instead, they let the spirit of the FirstBeast move among them, and give them evil counsel. Then brother turned against sister, and father against child, for they all desired to lead the Great Pack. When the OldMother saw this, she was greatly displeased, and she sent her chosen one, GreyMane, to set us back on the scent of righteousness."

Several of the other converts had by now picked up on the rhythm of the sermon, and they shouted, "Have mercy on us, OldMother!"

LifeCrier acknowledged the response with a slight nod and resumed. "But hard were the hearts of those first kin, and blind were their eyes to truth. GreyMane's brother was full of the spirit of the FirstBeast, and the pack stood behind him as he ripped the life from her throat. Then did the OldMother fall on the Great Pack, her hackles as tall as great trees, her fangs gleaming like the sun. With thunder and fire, she drove the kin from the Forest of Dawn and scattered them to the winds, to suffer and die in the world until their children's children's children had paid the price of their sins." LifeCrier paused for a breath.

The converts yelled their enthusiastic responses.

Slowly, lovingly, LifeCrier looked over the crowd. His ears relaxed; his expression softened. In a gentler tone of voice, he continued. "Thus has it been for a thousand generations. We are born. We suffer. We die. Our pups go hungry, our old ones fall victim to the sharpfangs, and our best and brightest hunters fight tooth and claw for the right to lead, for but a summer or two. While through the ages, the faithful have waited for the sign that we are at last forgiven. Through flood and famine, through the raging fires of autumn and the bitter frosts of winter, even when hope seemed as hard to find as a redwing's teeth, generations of kin have lived and died in the belief that the OldMother would send the Chosen One again, and we would once again live in harmony in the Forest of Dawn.

"Some have said that the believers were fools. Some have said that we waited in vain." LifeCrier paused to look the crowd over one more time, an enigmatic smile playing on his lips. The only sound from the converts was a disorganized mumble.

Then the old kin puffed his chest, raised his ears, and loosed a joyous bark. "Brethren, friends, members of the Great Pack: I am here today to tell you that the wait has *not* been in vain. For I bring you good news; the Chosen One *has* been sent among us, and her name is SilverSides!"

The crowd went up in another tumult of yipping and barking. Strained shouts of "Praise the OldMother!" mingled with shouts of "Praise SilverSides!" For a moment, watching the fervor of the crowd, WhiteTail wondered if her father really had any idea of the kind of energy he'd tapped. Then she put the question out of her mind. There were enough little problems to handle without confronting the big one.

"Listen. Listen!" In a bit, the crowd settled down again, and LifeCrier continued. "Look around you. Look at your neighbors. A year ago, this humble place, this PackHome, was a desperate and dying place. Hemmed in by other packs, we faced an invasion from the Hill of Stars. The WalkingStones were terrible enemies: Tall and swift, able to kill with a glance, they were as deadly as silent sharpfangs and twice as hard to kill. The game was driven away, and our young hunters were slain without honor. If ever there was a place that needed the OldMother, surely PackHome was it.

"Now, some have said that the OldMother has grown deaf to the cries of the kin, and her heart has long since hardened against us. But brethren, I am here to tell you that she listens to us still. For the OldMother heard the lamentations of PackHome; she saw the hungry pups, she smelled the unburied dead. The OldMother's heart was moved, and in our darkest hour she sent us her sign and her help, and the name was *SilverSides.*"

LifeCrier's voice dropped to a whisper. Remarkably, the crowd fell silent to listen. For a moment all WhiteTail heard was the wind rustling the leaves of the whitetrees and the distant call of a lonely bluecrest.

"I was *there*, oh my brethren," LifeCrier whispered. "You and I, we were born from our mothers. But the mother of SilverSides is the OldMother, who lives in the sky, and

SilverSides was born from a fiery star. These old eyes *saw* her come down from the sky, trailing flame and glory.

"She was as a cub, but she was formed fully grown. As soon as she could move, she felled a mighty sharpfang with one bite." LifeCrier looked around the clearing, gauging his audience's disbelief. "With one bite, brethren. Even before she could speak, she saved an entire hunting pack. And when she could at last speak, did she challenge KeenEye for the leadership of the hunt, as was her right under the law of the FirstBeast?

"No. She said, 'I am here to serve you.'"

He paused to let that thought sink in and catch his breath. After a few quick pants, he resumed speaking in his normal voice. "That is the first lesson, O members of the Great Pack. She accomplished great things; she fought with valor. But all these things she did to *serve* the pack.

"She hunted with the pack, and she was a mighty hunter. She led us against the WalkingStones, and drove them back in defeat." He leapt to his hind feet and held his amulet high. The sunlight twinkled and flashed on the broken circuit board. "This is the token she gave me, to remind me of my faith. It is a piece of the brain of a WalkingStone, and it does not decay!"

LifeCrier flashed the amulet around so all could see it. When the wondrous gasps had settled down, he hung the amulet around his neck again and dropped down to all fours. "That was just one of her miracles. There were many more, and in time I will tell you about them. But for now—for you who are taking your first trots down the path of faith—I leave you with these four promises, which she gave unto me. Let these be the four legs upon which your faith stands:

"SilverSides will protect us.

"SilverSides will serve us.

"SilverSides came once, to awaken us.

"SilverSides will come again, to lead us back to the Forest of Dawn."

Abruptly, LifeCrier turned and began descending from the rocky knoll. The crowd exploded in a tumult of barking and howling. Shouts of "Praise LifeCrier!" went up from one side of the clearing, and "Praise SilverSides!" from the other. A small fight started in the back when someone tried to shout "Praise the OldMother!" and the younglings in the front were swept aside by a mob of converts rushing forward to touch the fur of LifeCrier.

Unnoticed in all the noise and confusion, WhiteTail carefully worked her way around to the back side of the knoll. She paused only a moment, to think, *I sure hope I know what I'm doing*. Then in one quick dash she scampered to the top of the knoll and let rip with her best blood-curdling shriek.

Amazingly, the rabble all froze and stared at her.

Here goes nothing. WhiteTail flashed a wide, joyous, utterly fraudulent smile, whipped her tail excitedly, and barked out, "Hear me! I am WhiteTail, daughter of LifeCrier!"

"Praise LifeCrier!" the scruffy one near the front shouted.

She beamed at the crowd again. *Whatever you do, girl, don't make eye contact with your father*. "LifeCrier has asked me to make an announcement." She felt the fur on the back of her head prickle and knew that her father was staring at her. She could easily visualize his baffled expression as he tried to figure out what she was up to this time, and she started to glance in his direction. *Don't look at him!*

"In honor of this happy occasion," WhiteTail barked, "LifeCrier wishes it known that he himself will lead the first hunt of the Great Pack! He goes to the forest now; all who would truly follow in the footsteps of SilverSides, follow LifeCrier!" The pack erupted in a maelstrom of baying and hunting howls and surged forward to engulf LifeCrier.

Now, girl. Now you can look at him. WhiteTail picked her father's face out of the mob at the foot of the knoll. For an instant he looked back at her with daggers flashing in his eyes, and then he was swept away by the furry tide that streamed out into the forest. *Okay, Father*, WhiteTail thought with a snicker, *let's see you wriggle your way out of* this *one*. Bounding down from the knoll, she blended into the crowd and followed.

All her efforts were concentrated on keeping track of her father. She never noticed the small, green observation robot that drifted along at treetop level, following her.

Dr. Anastasi charged up the slidewalk from the tunnel transit stop, pinwheeled through a lobby, and caught the next flight of slidewalk. "Look at this, Basalom. Have you ever seen such conspicuous waste before?"

The First and Second Laws of Robotics prevented him from responding with an untruth, but Basalom deduced from experience that his mistress did not want a completely truthful answer. He kept his silence as he strode a respectful three paces behind her, but he carried on an internal dialogue. *Actually, Dr. Anastasi, we've both seen something exactly like this. Or have you forgotten the Ceremyons already?*

Dr. Anastasi rapped her knuckles on a ceiling support beam as the slidewalk rose up through the next floor. "Good grief. Iron. Chrome steel. Petrochemical plastics. They must have torn down an entire mountain to build this place."

"Quite possibly, madam." *Although in that case the scanning team would have spotted something beyond a little thermal pollution, no?*

Dr. Anastasi shook her head. "When I think of all the ecological damage that these things must cause—

"I mean, think of it, Basalom. Thousands of hectares of biosphere flattened, graded, and rendered utterly sterile. Entire species displaced." She turned around and took in the building

65

with a sweeping gesture. "You know, I think I've figured it out. The Robot Cities are fire ant nests. Enormous fire ant nests."

The allusion was a bit obscure; it took Basalom almost 30 nanoseconds to cross-reference and make the connection. *Fire ant: Solenopsis saevissima richteri. A fiercely stinging omnivorous ant native to the American continents of Earth, commonly thought responsible for the Great Agricultural Failure of the early 21st century. See North American History, Populist Rising of 2014.* Then he realized that Janet was obviously waiting for him to ask her to explain. "Fire ants, madam?"

"Nasty little brown bugs, native to Earth. Every now and then someone accidentally exports them to a Settler world.

"All it takes is one queen, at the start. But her offspring build these huge, networked, almost indestructible nests, strip the land of everything that can be eaten, and kill or drive out all the native species right up to cattle. Pretty soon, instead of a meadow, you've got a couple hectares of solid fire ant nest. And then they send out hordes of flying queens to start new colonies."

The slidewalk rose through another floor, and Janet looked around. "Yes, fire ants get established someplace, you may as well nuke the whole mess and start over."

They'd reached the top of the slidewalk. Janet wheeled and charged through an enormous open archway; Basalom followed an instant later, in time to see Dr. Anastasi get grabbed by two large, matte-black security robots.

His First Law reaction was immediate and overwhelming. *Dr. Anastasi is being attacked. I must defend her.*

Even as he started to move, within nanoseconds, secondary observations came into his central thought processor. The security robots were standard Robot City Avernus models: massive, solid, four meters tall, equipped with ominous-looking pincer hands—in short, far more menacing than the older "Gort" models found doing most security work on Spacer worlds. *These robots are subject to the First Law just as I am. Dr. Anastasi is in no danger. Perhaps they are restraining her in order to prevent her from entering an area of greater potential harm.*

Dr. Anastasi's face flushed red to the roots of her blond hair,

and she pounded ineffectually on the robot's broad metal chest.
"Put me down!"

"This is a restricted area," the robot said in a voice that
sounded like ball bearings in a blender.

"This is Central Hall. It can't be a restricted area."

The robot tilted its massive, helmet-like head back and
scanned her face. "You are not in my permissions file. Access
denied. If you would like to apply for permission—"

"Shut up!" She thumped the black behemoth on the side of
the head, and it responded by shifting its grip so that she could
no longer move her arms.

Casually, Basalom strolled into view, stopped a foot short
of the security robots' reaction perimeter, and opened a commlink channel. *Hello. Is there some problem here?*

This is a restricted area, the unoccupied security robot said.
Interestingly, its commlink signal projected the same gravelly
tone as the other's voice synthesizer.

Ah, I see. He looked at Dr. Anastasi as if curious. *What did
she do?*

*She attempted to enter the restricted zone without correct
permission.*

Dr. Anastasi caught her breath again. "Put me down, you
ugly tin lunkhead!"

Basalom nodded sagely. *And you stopped her. Good work.
But tell me, why is this zone restricted?*

*To prevent the risk of further attacks on Central. This one
fit the profile of a potential attacker.* Dr. Anastasi got a foot
loose and gave the security robot a good solid kick in the knee
joint. The hall echoed with the clang.

Basalom nodded again. *Indeed she does.* He looked back to
the security robot. *However, I'm curious about something. Who
issued the orders restricting this area?*

The Supervisory Council.

I see. And they're all robots, is that correct?

Yes.

Basalom stepped a bit closer, as if to examine Janet, but still
stayed circumspectly outside the security robot's reaction perimeter. *You are aware, of course, that this is a human.*

Both security robots responded. *Of course.* The one holding

Dr. Anastasi continued, *That is why I am restraining her without harming her.*

Basalom stepped back and looked the black robot straight in the oculars. *Under the Second Law, an order given by a human supersedes an order given by a robot—even by a robot on the Supervisory Council.*

Protection of Central stems directly from our fundamental programming, which was installed by the human Dr. Avery. The security robot hesitated, but persisted. *This security detail is therefore following a human order of higher priority.*

Basalom shifted his approach. *Dr. Anastasi is a former colleague of Dr. Avery's.* True enough, as far as it went. Basalom felt no need to amplify the relationship. *She is no danger to Central. In any case, human reactions are so slow compared to robots that you or I could stop her if she attempted an assault on Central. Besides, her order is direct and immediate, and is a situation not foreseen by your programming.* Also true enough. *I suggest you start obeying her orders.*

Security robots could be a bit thick, but even they eventually caught on. *Oh.*

Janet shrieked, "Let me go!" The robot holding her did, and she hit the floor with a plop. In an instant Basalom was at her side, helping her to her feet. All her attention was fixed on the security robot; the only notice she took of Basalom was to mutter, "You just have to know how to talk to these things."

"Indeed, madam."

Getting to her feet, Dr. Anastasi straightened her clothes and fixed the security robots with a steely glare. "Well, I hope you two have learned your lesson. Come along, Basalom." Though the security robots were both a good two meters taller than Janet, she brushed them aside and ploughed straight ahead into Central Hall.

Basalom followed her. One of the security robots started to open his commlink channel to challenge Basalom's security clearance, but Basalom struck first. *Implied Second Law: Dr. Anastasi has ordered me to accompany her. Therefore, she wishes me to enter this area, and therefore, she obviously wishes you to allow me to pass.* The security robots were still trying to parse that one out when Basalom and Dr. Anastasi disappeared out of sight around the corner.

A few seconds later they stood in the atrium at the heart of Central, facing the massive black slab that held Central's console input/output devices. Basalom couldn't quite put a manipulator on it, but he felt a sense of vague disquiet in the presence of the great machine. There were annoying, itchy subsonics in the air, and a deep, unsteady thrumming on the 104-Mhz band. The positronic potentials rose in his brain, meshed, and pointed toward a fuzzy conclusion: Something was wrong. But what?

Dr. Anastasi grew impatient. She crossed her arms. She tapped a foot. She cleared her throat loudly. At last, Central's one red eye slowly came to life. Clicks and grating sounds emanated from its voice synthesizer, followed by a burst of white noise and a 60-cycle hum that slowly resolved into a word.

"Hmmm?"

Janet uncrossed her arms and stepped forward. "Central, I am Dr. Janet Anastasi, and I'm here to—"

"Good morning, Dr. Chandra," the machine said. "I'm looking forward to beginning my lessons."

Janet blinked, shook her head, and tried again. "Anastasi. My name is Anastasi. And I'm a little short on time, so—"

"Time," Central said, "is a convention shaped by the collective mind of all sentience. It has no objective meaning outside the vision."

Dr. Anastasi turned to Basalom. "Do you have any idea what he's talking about?"

Basalom tried a brief query on his commlink, but got nothing but static in reply. "No, madam."

Janet shrugged and turned back to Central. "One more time, then. My name is Janet Anastasi. I am a roboticist. Roughly a year ago, I left an experimental learning machine on the surface of this planet. Its mission was—"

Central's eye flared brightly, then dimmed again to extinction.

No answer was forthcoming; Central had gone back into sleep mode. Turning to Janet, Basalom found her staring at her feet and counting to a very high number. The situation was saved by the arrival of a tall, slender, pale blue robot built along the lines of the Avery Euler model.

The robot swept into the atrium and began talking in a harried, accelerated voice. "Hello, you must be Dr. Anastasi. Please accept my apologies for not meeting you at the spaceport. Your arrival caught us completely by surprise."

Janet looked up. "No, really?"

The city robot was unused to dealing with humans, and therefore not tuned to detect sarcasm. "Truly, I am City Supervisor 3. You may find it more convenient to address me as Beta. I was involved in a major research project, but I came as soon as I was able to delegate authority. If it is necessary, my fellow supervisors can be summoned as well. You may consider the entire city to be at your disposal."

Janet looked around the hall and thought about the many meanings of the word *disposal*. "Thank you. To be honest— Beta, is it?—I don't want to spend any more time here than I absolutely must. I only came here to get one question answered.

"Before I ask it, though, I've got a new one. What the deuce is going on with Central?"

Beta's eyes dimmed, and he shuffled his feet nervously. Basalom detected a slight leakage of sadness on the commlink channel. "Central has been . . . *damaged*," Beta said.

"No kidding. What happened?"

"A rogue robot invaded the hall and attacked Central." Beta looked up. "You must understand, this was before we realized the need for tight security measures."

Janet absent-mindedly rubbed her upper arm. "Yes, I've met your security measures. But back up a moment: You said a rogue robot? No offense intended, but I've never heard of a rogue robot before, much less a rogue Avery robot."

"This was not an Avery robot."

Janet was suddenly stricken with a nasty, sinking feeling. "What kind of robot was it?"

Beta's eyes flashed, and he looked to Basalom for a moment. "We are not certain. It was not a design that we were familiar with. For example, it was constructed of a cellular material similar to our own, but of a much finer grain. And, while it was subject to the Laws of Robotics, it seemed to have no clear idea of what constituted a human."

Basalom switched to commlink. *Stand by for download of data.* When Beta had acknowledged, Basalom transmitted a summary of the learning machine's design specification. *Was this the robot that attacked Central?*

Why, yes. Then on audio, Beta repeated, "Yes, that's it. The rogue robot was a unit of the type you describe as a learning machine. This explains a lot of things."

Janet grabbed Beta and turned him to face her. "Like *what?* Exactly what did the rogue robot do?"

Beta's eyes flashed again, and there was a hesitation in his voice. "Dr. Anastasi, the rogue apparently became convinced that it was a member of the local species. It assumed their form. It took over leadership of a small socio-political unit. From what we have been able to establish lately, it has apparently been adopted by that unit as a minor deity."

Janet let go of Beta and sagged. "Frost . . ."

"The learning machine led repeated attacks against Robot City. It destroyed several hunter/seekers, a number of worker robots, and City Supervisor Gamma on two different occasions. Ultimately, it attempted to destroy Central."

Janet sat down on the floor and buried her face in her hands. "Frost, frost, f—" She looked up and grabbed Beta's knee. "*What happened to it?*"

"Master Derec—are you familiar with the human called Derec, also known as David Avery?"

Janet smiled at the mention of her son. "Oh, I've heard of him."

"Master Derec arrived and convinced the rogue that he was human. It took the form of a fairly normal robot, and has since left the planet as part of Master Derec's entourage."

Frowning at Basalom, Dr. Anastasi got to her feet and began straightening her hair. "Well, I suppose that's the best we could hope for. At least it isn't destroyed." She turned to Beta. "You say the learning machine assumed leadership of the primitive sentients?"

"Yes, madam. Our current research project involves studying the primitives. From what we have been able to decode of their language, it appears that primitives now regard the learning machine as a messiah figure. It has caused considerable disruption to their social order."

Dr. Anastasi stroked her chin. "I see. So now you're looking for a way to undo the damage?"

"No, madam. We have concluded that the disruption is too significant for us to repair. Instead, we are seeking ways to take advantage of it, in order to persuade the natives to take up residence in the city."

"What?"

Beta blithely continued. "Robot City exists to serve humans. Since there are no humans in permanent residence on this world, we have concluded that the intelligent primitives are human equivalents, or near-humans. Therefore, in order for us to protect and serve them, they must take up residence in the city."

Janet went back to staring at her feet and counting to high numbers. Basalom switched to thermographic vision and noted that Mount Anastasi was building up to another eruption.

Janet said, "Next I suppose you're going to tell me that this is for their own good."

"Of course, madam. Our observations have shown that the near-humans live in a dirty, dangerous environment. If they can be persuaded to accept some changes, we can make their lives much more pleasant."

This time, Janet defused the angry outburst herself. "Okay, Basalom. Contact the ship. Tell it we're going to be staying here for a while. We may as well try to steer these tin fascists onto a constructive path." Basalom opened his commlink channel and did as Dr. Anastasi instructed.

While he was still on the commlink, though, he intercepted a coded transmission intended for Beta. The code was a simple one, composed of prime number transpositions, and Basalom cracked it in about 50 nanoseconds. He was just in time to catch Beta's answering transmission.

Go ahead, Linguist 6.

We have been engaged by a hunting party of near-humans. Supervisor Gamma has already been destroyed.

Again? Very well; try to salvage his brain, if they'll let you.

That may be difficult. Biologist 42 is down with a damaged leg, Organic Chemist 20 is locked up in a First Law dilemma, and I've lost my left arm below the elbow.

Understood. Mission aborted. Return to the city.

Will comply if possible. The near-humans are circling back. They've cut us off. I don't think we're going to make it. We'd

*better upload our observational data now. Stand by for core
dump.*

Ready.

I am commencing to trans—

After that, there was only static.

CHAPTER 11
MAVERICK

A forest glen: sunlight filtered cool and green through the leaves, while nesting redwings darted through the lower branches of the trees, piping cheerfully. High in the canopy above a newly emerged cicabeetle announced its successful pupation with a loud, low-pitched drone, and off in the distance the happy cries and howls of hunting kin echoed across the valley.

The bowl-shaped floor of the forest clearing was covered with rocky outcroppings, mossy old stumps and fallen logs, and the mangled remains of four robots.

A skinny youngling sauntered past, proudly carrying his prize by the wires that had once connected it to a neck. Someone on the other side of the clearing shouted, distracting the youngling; he dropped City Supervisor Gamma's head onto a slab of exposed rock, and the resulting clang sent him scampering away. By the time the youngling realized what he'd done and turned back to retrieve the head, it had begun rolling down the slope. Picking up momentum, it skittered across a patch of wet slimewort, dinged off a jutting rock, and took an off-kilter hop and then a long, wobbling bounce. The youngling bounded down the slope after it, trying to catch up with the rolling head.

He skidded to a stop when the head thudded to rest in a pile of soft humus and rotting leaves at the base of a mossy tree stump, not half a trot in front of the tough-looking stranger's nose.

The head apparently annoyed the stranger. He got to his feet, yawned, and cast a baleful glare at the youngling. Then he sniffed the head in a disinterested fashion, marked it with his scent, and sat down again.

The youngling decided to go find another trophy.

Maverick watched the young kin turn tail, then turned his attention back to the head. *So that was a WalkingStone, eh? Big furry deal. It wasn't so tough.* He brought a hind paw up and indulged in a good scratch behind the ear and resumed picking at the bit of grainy material that was stuck between his front teeth. *On the other paw, I can't say much for the way they taste.* Dislodging the shred of Linguist 6's arm, he spat it out and turned his attention to the group of kin that was busy dismembering the last relatively intact carcass. WhiteTail was easy to spot.

And that's the old guy's daughter, huh? Yuck. She's got spindly legs. Walks like she's got starch in her tail. And she's a bit young, even for your tastes.

Still, what the hey. Maybe in a year or two she'll turn into something worth howling about. And in the meantime, let's not lose sight of why we came here. The old guy's in charge, and he depends on her. Offpaw, I'd say that she's definitely the angle to work, for now. Maverick yawned again, in a deliberately casual way, and gave the rest of the clearing a once-over.

On the whole, he had to admit that this group hunt business hadn't turned out too badly. At first it'd looked like something straight out of one of his worst nightmares: A chaotic mob of two hundred clumsy pack-kin charging through the briars and stingworts, barking and howling loud enough to send even a deaf *smerp* running for cover.

But by the time they'd gone a hundred trots from PackHome, the mob had started to break up. Somebody who actually knew something about hunting caught a whiff of a smallgrazer and led a split off on that trail. A bunch of younglings treed a nuteater and stayed behind to bark like fools, jump around a lot, and prove once again that kin can't climb trees, no matter how hard they try.

Other groups splintered off to chase other promising scents, but Maverick kept his eyes on LifeCrier. There had been a lot of twists, turns, and feints—for a moment there he'd had the absurd idea that LifeCrier was trying to ditch them all and sneak back to PackHome—but even though his left hind leg had started to throb, he'd managed to stick with the old kin the entire way.

After all, that was the whole point of coming to PackHome, wasn't it? To find the center of power, get close to it, and work your way up in the pecking order. And up to a certain point, the plan really had seemed to be working. The group following LifeCrier was down to fewer than ten kin when they'd burst from the underbrush and run straight into the pack of WalkingStones.

Maverick let out a disgusted little sneeze. *WalkingStones? You mean the horrible, nasty, killer monsters that we need SilverSides to protect us from? Mother, I've seen trees that put up a better fight!* Despite all the scary talk about silent death and glances that killed, there'd been no lightning, and no thunder. The WalkingStones had simply stood there on their hind legs, staring at the onrushing kin, looking for all the world like a bunch of startled whistlepigs caught out in the sunlight.

If LifeCrier had shown even a second's hesitation, that would have been the end of it. *But the old fool obviously believes this SilverSides business. He charged right in.*

And OldMother help me, I followed him. One of the WalkingStones had started to point its left foreleg at LifeCrier. Maverick really hadn't had time to think, or even slow down; he'd feinted, stutter-stepped, and charged straight for the WalkingStone.

It was a good gamble, Mavvy old boy. If the stories about them throwing lightning from their paws are true, you saved the old guy's life. That could have been a real good play, gratitude-wise. With a mighty grunt, he'd gathered himself and sprung upon the WalkingStone, seizing its foreleg in his jaws.

That's where everything had gone wrong. Biting the WalkingStone's limb was like biting gravel. Between the cold pain in his teeth, the oily and utterly unappetizing taste of the

WalkingStone's flesh, and the apparent lack of any bones in the limb, Maverick had momentarily forgotten everything that he knew about balance and timing. He'd been counting on his momentum to pull the WalkingStone off its two feet, just as he'd been counting on its inertia to check his leap.

Instead, the thing's foreleg had simply torn away in his teeth and he'd gone flying head-over-haunches into a patch of blooming stingwort. His heroic leap had ended up as a clumsy pratfall.

Maverick looked around the clearing again—a clearing full of kin who were *not* noticing him—and felt a sense of frustration. *It's definitely darned tough to impress the locals by landing flat on your tailbone.*

Of course, I suppose it could be worse. Though at the moment it's hard to imagine how.

Between getting the wind knocked out of him and giving his sore leg a bad twist, he'd managed to take himself out of the fight for a few minutes. By the time he'd crawled out of the stingworts and gotten back up on all four legs, the battle was over. Old LifeCrier was up on a rock giving a victory benediction (though Maverick had to admit that the old kin *did* look a bit pale and shaky), the younglings were doing an extremely sloppy job of skinning and dressing the downed carcasses, and WhiteTail was busy braiding a bunch of those silly little amulets, like the one LifeCrier wore, and handing them out to the kin who'd managed to stay in the thick of the fight.

His gaze locked on WhiteTail again, and he allowed himself a wry smile. *Okay, Mavvy old boy, so much for coming into PackHome like a conquering hero. Guess it's time to try Plan B: Fall in love with the leader's daughter.* He groomed his fur a little bit, straightened up his shoulders, and started rehearsing his opening line. Then he gave WhiteTail one last appraising look, and grimaced. *All the same, her legs* are *spindly. Oh, the things I do for my meals.* Pasting a cheerful smile on his face, he started his tail going in a slow, friendly wag and sauntered over.

The rest of the younglings had wandered off, dragging the detachable parts of the last WalkingStone with them. WhiteTail was squatting beside the now headless torso, carefully stripping out the thin, tough veins that were threaded throughout its chest cavity. She seemed to be picking them out on the basis of color;

the impression was reinforced when she measured out three equal lengths of yellow, green, and black vein and quickly braided them into a necklace.

With deliberate casualness, Maverick sat down and watched her work, an interested expression on his face. When she failed to notice him after a minute or so, he discreetly cleared his throat and wagged his tail a bit more vigorously.

She looked up; their eyes met for an instant. No sparks flew. She went back to her work.

So much for love at first sniff. Mavvy old boy, you're going to have to talk to her. After a few moments of silence, he cleared his throat again and spoke up. "Praise SilverSides."

"Praise SilverSides," she answered, without looking up or slowing her work.

Okay, Mavvy, let's turn on the charm. "Say, WhiteTail, can you believe that fight? We took four WalkingStones down and didn't even get singed. I tell you, SilverSides must be watching over us for sure."

WhiteTail paused in her work long enough to fix Maverick with a strange look. "Do I know you?"

The question caught Maverick by surprise. "Well, no. I mean, er——"

WhiteTail's ears went up, and she leaned in closer to sniff at Maverick. "Still, there's something familiar about you." She sniffed again, and then her eyes narrowed just a hair. "Oh, I remember now. You were in the front row at the meeting, weren't you?"

Okay, lad, there's your opening! Maverick leaned back a bit, puffed his chest slightly, and gave her an easy smile. "As a matter of fact, I was. Fascinating sermon, simply fascinating. Your father is——"

"You were the one who kept jumping in early on the cheering, weren't you?"

Oops. Maverick's ears went flat. "Er, actually——"

WhiteTail set her knife aside, sat up alertly, and looked closely at Maverick. "Yes, I remember now. Did you know that I was watching you almost the entire time?"

Maverick's ears popped up straight. "You *were?*"

WhiteTail turned back to the carcass, but not before shooting one last look of disgust at Maverick. "Did you really think that you were the first one to try to improve your status by loudly faking belief?''

"Fake? Look here, girl, I—'' The argument died in his throat.

Face it, Mavvy old boy, she's a very clever one, and she's got you by the ears. You may as well try the truth. Maverick plopped down on his belly, crossed his forepaws, and laid his chin on his paws. "Okay, I admit it. Every pack I've ever met has their own kind of strangeness, and I thought this SilverSides business was just one more weird local custom. I've been on my own for over a year, and I'm getting really tired of being an outcast. Can you blame me for trying too hard to fit in?''

WhiteTail set her knife aside again and favored Maverick with a less enigmatic smile. "You get two points for honesty, stranger. Most fakers just protest louder when they're caught. You're the first one I've met who's shown even a vestige of integrity.

"In return for that, I'll give you a little confession of my own. I don't believe, either.'' WhiteTail's eyes narrowed, and she watched him closely, studying his reaction.

Well, Mavvy, this honest bit seems to be getting us somewhere. Let's go with it. Maverick sat up, cocked his head sideways, raised one ear, and gave WhiteTail a bewildered look. "You don't? But at the meeting you said—I mean . . .''

WhiteTail's expression hardened. "Understand one thing, stranger. LifeCrier isn't just the leader of PackHome, he's my father, and I'll do whatever it takes to protect him. That includes tricking him into leading a hunt when the pack is hungry.'' With a swiftness that surprised Maverick, WhiteTail suddenly snatched up her stone knife and set its point against his breast-bone. "Or cutting your heart out and feeding it to the sharpfangs if you try your pious-believer act on him. Do I make myself clear?''

Gingerly, Maverick pushed the point aside. "Absolutely.''

"Good.'' She dropped her guard and turned her attention back to the carcass. "Now either get lost or make yourself useful. Do you know anything about WalkingStone anatomy?''

Maverick followed her gaze down into the jumbled pale blue mess that was the inside of the WalkingStone's chest cavity. Judging by color, there were at least six different kinds of veins, but the cavity was strangely bloodless and there was nothing that he could clearly identify as a heart. For that matter, he wasn't even sure that he could tell the difference between organ and muscle. A lot of the cavity was filled with the oily blue gravel he'd been picking out of his teeth since the fight.

"No," he finally admitted.

"Good. Here's your chance to learn. Help me roll this thing over, will you?" With a grunt of exertion, WhiteTail started pushing at the corpse. Maverick helped her. Despite being legless and headless, the corpse was surprisingly heavy, but together they managed to get it flipped.

"Now, stranger—" She looked up sharply. "Say, what *is* your name, anyway?"

He hesitated a moment. *Well, boy, just how far do we want to push this honesty business?* "Maverick," he said at last.

"Maverick? That's an outcast name. Don't you have a pack name?"

He looked away, and his tail started twitching in tight, nervous jerks. "Not any more."

WhiteTail gave him another appraising look and then shrugged. "Pay attention; I don't like to repeat myself." She picked up her knife and turned to the corpse.

"Now," WhiteTail began in a cool, formal voice, "the problem with hunting for WalkingStones is that there doesn't seem to be anything inside them that we can *eat*." She dug her knife in between where the shoulder blades should have been—if the thing had had bones—and opened the carcass down the back. By this time it was no longer surprising to find that the WalkingStone had no spine.

"They have no liver," WhiteTail continued. "No heart, no kidneys, and the muscles—well, you've already tried a leg. What did you think?"

Maverick grimaced at the memory. "I'd rather eat a stinktail."

WhiteTail nodded sagely. "A popular opinion." She caught Maverick's eye and directed it to the WalkingStone's shoulder area. "Another problem is that the WalkingStones don't seem to have a proper skin. It's impossible to tell where the skin ends and the muscle begins—which makes it really funny to watch the younglings try to flay one of them.

"But there's something else even more peculiar about the skin that I want you to see. Look there; what's happening?"

Maverick got up on all fours and sniffed closely at the spot WhiteTail had indicated. "Why, it's *healing.*"

WhiteTail frowned helplessly. "This WalkingStone is dead, right? I mean, its front legs are over here, its back legs are—" she looked around the clearing a bit and gestured in the direction of a fallen log, "—over there, I think. And Mother knows where the head's gotten to.

"But leave the skin alone for a few minutes, and wounds flow closed so fast you can watch it. Leave the *organs* alone long enough, and they melt down into this gritty blue stuff that's indistinguishable from skin or muscle." WhiteTail dug the knife in again and extended the cut across the Walking-Stone's hip area.

"So far as we can tell, there are only two organs in a WalkingStone that don't change shape. One is the brain. The other—" she plunged her forepaws into the wound and began groping around inside the body "—is usually right about—" a slightly startled look flashed across her face, and then resolved into a smile "—here!" With a sucking, popping sound, the corpse gave up the organ, and WhiteTail fell over backward with the recoil.

Maverick looked at the thing she'd gone to so much work to pull out. "A giant egg?"

"That's what it looks like, all right." WhiteTail got back on her feet, brushed some of the clinging blue grit off the thing, and then found her knife and tapped the egg a few times with the blade. "But it's got the hardest shell that I have ever seen."

Maverick wrinkled his nose in a deep frown. "Still, an *egg?*"

"Interesting thought, isn't it? That WalkingStones might be some kind of giant flyer? Although personally I think the shape and size is more like a sharpfang egg."

Maverick shook his head. "No."

WhiteTail tapped the egg with her knife again. "Agreed, sharpfang eggs are soft and leathery, while this one is as hard as a rock, and too small. Still—"

Maverick pushed in and laid a paw on the egg. "No, you don't understand. These four WalkingStones we killed; they

all carried eggs?'' WhiteTail nodded. Maverick looked her
straight in the eyes. ''Don't you see?''

WhiteTail didn't see. ''What?''

''No wonder they were such poor fighters. We jumped a
bunch of females who were all *nesting*.''

The instant those words left his lips, Maverick knew he'd
made a mistake. Whatever warmth had been in WhiteTail's
eyes, it was gone now. She drew herself up to her full, slender
height and asked, ''And tell me, O great hunter, since when
is a mother protecting her young harmless?''

''Well,'' Maverick hedged, ''there are some; female whistlepigs, and redflyers too, and . . .''

''Useless, absolutely useless,'' WhiteTail growled. ''I
shouldn't be wasting my time with you.''

Maverick froze, rooted to the spot, as his internal voices
erupted into a full-scale screaming argument.

Submit, idiot, submit!

What? To this *insolent little pup?*

Who also happens to be the leader's daughter!

*Don't do it, lad. Roll over and bare your throat to her now
and you'll never get another chance to show her who rules the
den.*

But you were wrong, *idiot!*

''Well?'' WhiteTail said in challenge.

Maverick was saved by the arrival of LifeCrier, who blithely
trotted right between them. ''Okay you two lovebirds, break
it up. We've still got a day's hunting ahead of us.'' A few trots
away, he looked over his shoulder without breaking stride and
added, ''Well, daughter? Are you coming?''

WhiteTail's hackles went down, her lips relaxed back down
over her fangs, and she turned to follow him. ''Yes, Father.''
Maverick started breathing again, and he turned his back to
WhiteTail and took another look at the egg.

The bite on his hindquarters took him completely by surprise.

''*Yike!*'' He leapt half a trot in the air and came down in a
whirl. WhiteTail was standing there with a wicked smile on
her face and a little bit of his fur in her teeth. ''What was *that*
for?'' he demanded.

''Just a reminder, *sweetheart*. I'm not done with you yet.''

Then, with a cold glare and a vicious snap of her whip-like tail, she turned and trotted after her father.

Maverick sat down and watched her go. When she was safely out of earshot, he softly said, ''Mavvy old boy, are you sure you want to be in the same pack with her?''

Five minutes later, when LifeCrier had gathered all the other adult hunters and gotten them formed up and ready to move out, Maverick still hadn't come up with an answer to that question. So he took one last look at the WalkingStone egg— only to discover that a skinny youngling had dragged it off, wedged it in a crevice, and started pounding on it with a rock. Then he sighed, got to his feet, and trotted after the rest of the pack.

Had he understood that the egg was actually Linguist 6's microfusion power pod, he would have moved considerably faster.

CHAPTER 12
DEREC

Derec and his father sat side by side in the ship's robotics lab, hunched over a matching pair of robotic data entry terminals, staring intently at the video displays. A casual observer might have mistaken the pair of them for a new breakthrough in humaniform robots, so still were they: unmoving, except for their fingers and the barely perceptible motions of their chests as they breathed; unblinking, their paired attention completely focused on their work.

And yet there was something subtle, barely tangible, yet almost unmistakably *lifelike* about the pair. It wasn't the white stubble on Avery's chin; that effect could have been achieved with common nylon bristle. Perhaps it was the delicate filigree of bloodshot veins that adorned the whites of Derec's eyes. More likely it was his hair, which had that limp, greasy look that could only be achieved through the use of expensive petrochemical plastics.

Or three days of nonstop programming.

Occasionally, a finger moved. Lips parted; a word or two passed between them, although not in anything that the average observer would have recognized as being part of a human conversation.

"Adb ixform."

"Got it."

"0B09?"

"15."

"0B2C?"

"A0."

"Sounds good." There was a long pause while Avery studied something on his screen.

Whatever it was caused him to frown and then to speak again. "Can you give me a du?"

"Fifteen-point-four-four-three-seven gigs."

"Well, if that's not enough, I don't know what is. Set the pipe."

"Piped."

Avery leaned back in his chair, ran his fingers through his bristly white hair, and blew out a deep breath. "Okay, we're as ready as we're ever going to be. Cross your fingers and start the yacc."

"Yaccing." Derec punched one last command into the terminal and leaned back in his chair in unconscious mimicry of his father. Numbers flashed and danced across the screen; Derec watched it for a few minutes and then rubbed his gritty eyes and turned to Avery. "Now what?"

"We wait." Slowly, painfully, Avery got up out of his chair and limped over to the autogalley. "Coffee, black," he told the machine.

Derec noticed the limp, and a reaction finally worked its way to his vocal cords. "You okay, Dad?" There was genuine concern in his voice.

Avery chuckled a little and slapped his dragging leg. "Yeah, I'm okay. Foot fell asleep, that's all."

"Oh." Derec yawned. The autogalley chimed gently, and the serving door slid open to reveal the cup of coffee that Avery had ordered. Derec's nose perked up at the rich, earthy scent. "Smells good," he observed.

"You want some?"

Derec thought it over. "Sure. With casein and two lumps of sugar."

"Decaf? You look like you could use some sleep."

Derec rubbed the back of his neck and then studied the grit that had adhered to his fingers. "Nah. I've been in here three days; Ari'll make me sleep on the couch anyway. May as well stay awake."

"Okay." Avery repeated Derec's order to the autogalley. When the second steaming cup appeared, he picked it up and carefully carried it over to the work table.

The two of them sat quietly for a few minutes, sipping their cups of coffee, while the numbers danced and capered across Derec's terminal display.

"I hate robotic coffee," Avery said at last.

Derec spoke without looking up. "Why?"

"Fresh-brewed coffee's supposed to burn your tongue. That way you take a little more time, drink it a little slower. Robot-made coffee is served lukewarm, gets cold too fast. You have to gulp it down and get back to work."

"Oh." Derec took another sip and resumed staring into space.

"I could use some food," Avery said after another long pause. "Anything you're partial to?" He got up again and toddled over to the autogalley.

Derec gave the matter his deepest available thought. "Snack food," he decided, with some effort. "Crackers. Cheese. Something along those lines."

Avery leaned against the bulkhead, rested a hand on the autogalley's control panel, and scrolled through the menu of preprogrammed selections. "Cheese is a pretty complex organic compound," he said. "I'd hate to taste what this thing might come up with if it's not specifically programmed for— ah, here we go. Magellanic *fromage*. Close enough for you?"

"Sure." Derec waved a hand in a noncommittal gesture. Avery gave the autogalley the order, and in a minute he returned to the table bearing a plate full of blue marbled paste and some little round white things that were either crackers or poker chips.

"Dig in, son." Avery smashed a chip into the mound of paste and stuffed the resulting accretion into his mouth. Derec picked up a dry cracker and began nibbling at it in an absent-minded manner.

A half-dozen goo-covered crackers later, Avery took a slurp of coffee and turned to Derec. "Well, any lint yet?"

Derec checked his terminal screen. "Nope."

Avery frowned. "I hate sitting through yaccs. I mean, I just feel like I should be doing *something* constructive with this time."

Derec looked up and gave his father a bleary-eyed stare. "Such as?"

"Oh, talking, maybe. Finding out the answers to some questions that have been bothering me for a long time."

Derec yawned. "Okay." There was a long pause. "Anything in particular you wanted to talk about?"

Avery closed his eyes, stroked his whiskery chin, and thought it over. "Yes," he decided. "This Aranimas fellow: Who is he, and why is he trying to kill you?"

Derec shrugged. "You want the full story or the condensed version?"

"Depends. Where's the yacc at?"

Derec rubbed his eyes and checked the terminal one more time. "About twenty percent, I'd guess."

"That far already? Better condense it."

"Okay." Derec took a deep slug of his coffee and closed his eyes in thought. Just when Avery was starting to wonder if he should give the boy a little nudge to wake him up, Derec opened his eyes and began speaking in a low, raspy voice.

"Aranimas is an alien, from somewhere outside Settler space. You could call him a humanoid, depending on how loosely you define human, but when I finally got a close look at him, the first thing I thought of was a plucked condor with fisheyes."

Derec took a nip of his cracker, chewed it thoughtfully, and swallowed. "His species call themselves the Erani. They're a wonderfully simple people: vicious, brutal, and utterly without empathy. In a couple years you'll be able to look up 'cruel' in the dictionary and see a picture of an Erani. You'd get along great with them." Derec paused to sip his now-cold coffee.

Avery bristled at the boy's cheap shot, but held his tongue.

"The Erani claim to control about two hundred worlds, but I think they must be counting every rock, asteroid, and moonlet in their solar system. That ship of his—did you happen to get a look at his ship before we jumped?" Avery shook his head. "Oh. Well, that ship of his appears to be one-of-a-kind, the first hyperdrive the Erani ever developed. I don't know whether Aranimas built it or stole it, but the first thing he did when he got to human space was hijack a good Auroran hull to put it in. Wolruf tells me the Erani hyperdrive is fantastically unstable, and that being in the engine room of their ship is almost as dangerous as being on the wrong end of their guns.''

Avery interrupted. ''What *is* Wolruf, anyway? A genetically engineered dog or something? And how'd you hook up with it?''

''Her,'' Derec corrected. ''No, Wolruf—that's not her real name, by the way, that's just as close as the human voice can pronounce it. I guess our mouths aren't the right shape, or we don't have the right ultrasonic frequency components in our speech and hearing to really get her name right.

''Anyway, Wolruf was Aranimas's navigator. She was basically a sort of indentured servant on board that ship; I counted at least four different species of intelligent aliens on board Aranimas's ship, and they were all conquered subjects of the Erani. I suspect that if we humans ever have a real confrontation with the Erani, we're going to find a lot of allies on their subject worlds. I met Wolruf when—

''But wait, I'm getting ahead of myself. Let me put this story in linear order, okay?'' Derec gave Avery a questioning stare; Avery didn't respond, so Derec finished off the last of his coffee and caught his breath.

''Now, this whole thing starts with that asteroid you dumped me on after you wiped my memory. You remember that asteroid?''

Avery looked down. ''I—I was insane then, Derec,'' he said softly. ''I'm not sure what I remember and what I hallucinated.''

''Well, I was still trying to figure out your asteroid when Aranimas showed up and started shooting the thing to pieces. You see, there's three things the Erani don't have: a fleet of hyperdrive ships, a key to Perihelion, and a glimmer of understanding about robotics. They have a slave culture, you see, and since organic slaves are free for the taking, they've had no incentive to develop mechanical ones.

''On the other hand, while they don't know a thing about robotics, they apparently know a lot more about hyperwave than we do. Aranimas was able to identify and *track* the hyperwave interference caused by a key to Perihelion.''

Derec abruptly realized that he'd been getting excited and lowered his voice. "That's what brought him to the asteroid. Once there, I guess he saw all those robots and decided to do a little old-fashioned Erani slave-raiding. It'd never occurred to him that the robots would self-destruct instead of surrendering. Capturing me was just an accidental bonus.

"Not that he was happy about it. Apparently he's been skulking around human space for a few years, hijacking the occasional ship and trying to pick up robots. When he captured me he was convinced that I'd cheated him out of a good load of slaves, and he—" Derec faltered a moment and winced at the memory of the torture he'd suffered at Aranimas's hands. "Let's just leave it at that, okay?" Derec found another cracker, loaded it up with Magellanic *fromage*, and resumed talking around the mouthful of cheese.

"Wolruf, as I said, was part of the crew. Ariel was a prisoner, although I didn't find that out for a while. Mandelbrot was a collection of junk parts in a locker."

Avery interrupted again. "Mandelbrot? Isn't he at least three-quarters Capek, Ariel's old valet robot from back on Aurora?"

Derec scowled at Avery. "Beats me. You gave me amnesia, remember?"

"Sorry. I forgot."

Derec took another bite of the cracker and continued. "Dad, I don't know what kind of crazy experiment you really had in mind when you dumped me on that asteroid—"

"I'm not sure I remember either," Avery muttered, "although I think I remember trying to explain it. But that may have been an hallucination. I *was* crazy."

"—but Aranimas had been doing his share to foul it up. By the time we got away from him, I had no memory, of course, and Ariel was losing hers to the amnemonic plague. I'd cobbled together Mandelbrot and programmed him with a pretty restrictive definition of human, which may have influenced some of the Robot City developments along that line. And Wolruf had finally gotten fed up with the Erani and decided to jump ship. With her help we got away while Aranimas was on a raid on a Spacer station, and then we had to steal the key to Perihe-

lion back from the robots before we could use it to escape—
and that's how we got to Robot City.''

Avery was silent. Derec ran his fingers through his greasy
hair, leaned forward, and shook his head.

"Y'know, Dad, as experiments go, yours didn't go too
well.''

Avery sighed and nodded. "No. No, it didn't, son, and
maybe someday I'll be able to apologize for putting you through
it. But right now it's just too big, and I have too much trouble
coming to grips with the idea that I actually *did* that to you.
I'm sorry.'' Then an idea hit Avery, and he frowned.

"But before I get too sorry, I'd like to remind you that you
still haven't answered my main question: Why is Aranimas *still*
trying to kill you?''

Derec shrugged. "An Erani never forgets.'' He helped himself to the last cracker and then looked at his terminal screen.
"Oops. We're just about done yaccing. Better finish that coffee
and get back to work.''

"Okay.'' Avery hurriedly drained the cup, tossed it into the
disposal chute, and then slipped into his chair.

Derec checked his screen again and turned to Avery. "Seriously, Aranimas is desperate for robots. That's why he follows me, I think; he knows that wherever I go, there are bound
to be lots of robots.

"I don't think he can comprehend the Three Laws, though.
I mean, he understands the words well enough, but I think the
idea that robots simply *can't* hurt humans is just too alien a
concept for him. Maybe it's too alien for *any* Erani.'' Derec
stole a sidelong glance at his terminal, and quickly spun back
to Avery to squeeze one last thought in.

"So here's an idea: If we ever find out where the Erani home
world is, what do you say we drop a half-dozen Robot Cities
on it? That ought to drive those ugly clowns just absolutely
crazy.''

Avery didn't have time to respond. The two data terminals
chimed simultaneously, then blanked and displayed the final
results of the yacc.

Both Avery and Derec immediately switched into zombie
programmer mode.

"Any lint?''

"No, it's clean."

"Okay, let's grep gen_shape."

"Grepping."

"A053?"

"15."

"A0C0?"

"AF."

"Very good. Nice it."

"Niced with a tee."

"Thanks, I forgot about that. Iostat?"

Derec paused a moment to page through several screens of data. "Clean, green, and five by five. I think it worked."

"Okay, let's finish it. Nohup."

"Nohupped."

"Chown gen_shape."

"Chowned."

Avery leaned back in his chair and crossed his fingers. "Here goes. I am putting ixform to sleep. Any floating children?"

Derec scrutinized his screen. "No—no, we're clear. No children floating in the pipe."

Avery suddenly realized that he'd been holding his breath. "Well! I think we've got it. Do you want to put it to the test?"

Derec smiled and waved an open hand at his father. "You, sir, may have the honor."

"Okay." Avery pushed his chair back from the terminal, tented his fingers, and frowned. Then he cleared his throat, raised his eyes to the ceiling, and said in a loud, clear voice: "Gosh, Derec, I think I need to use the Personal." Both of them locked their stares on Avery's chair.

Nothing happened. No softening around the edges; no reconfiguration of the seatpad. For over a minute they both held their breaths, waiting to see if the chair was going to reconfigure itself.

It remained a chair.

"Ya*hoo!*" Derec raised his fists in a victorious gesture, and Avery cracked into a broad, beaming smile. "Dad, we *did* it! We've cut out the autonomic shape-changing!"

Avery allowed himself another smile and then sobered. "We're halfway there, Derec. We made the changes we wanted. Now let's make sure that we haven't done any other damage in the process.'' He turned away from Derec, looked up at the ceiling, and loudly said, ''Ship, make this chair two inches higher.''

Smoothly and silently, as if it were a robobarber's chair, the seat rose two inches. Avery looked at Derec with a tight smile on his face and a merry twinkle in his eye. ''Son, we've cut out the autonomic routines, but we've kept the voluntary control intact. Now *that* is what I call a success.'' He hesitated a moment and then impulsively stuck out a hand to Derec.

For a moment, Avery felt terribly uncertain and insecure. Derec was looking at the hand as if he expected to find a joy-buzzer. Then he switched to looking Avery straight in the eye, with an unreadable expression on his face.

And then he smiled, reached over, and shook his father's hand. ''Congratulations, Dad.''

''Thanks, son.''

The moment passed. They broke off the handshake, both looking a little sheepish about their undisciplined display of raw emotion, and went back to their respective terminal displays.

''You know,'' Derec said at last, ''I'm beginning to feel that I really understand this polymorphism business.''

''That's just what I was thinking,'' Avery agreed.

''I mean, look at that pipe. It's totally tubular.''

''Totally.''

The two of them studied their displays a while longer, and then Derec spoke up. ''You know, as long as we're on such a good roll, we really should find something else to work on.''

''I quite agree.''

''Got any ideas?''

A wicked smile appeared on Avery's face. He tried to suppress it, but it could not be denied, so he turned it on Derec. ''Where did you say Lucius II was?''

Derec was aghast. ''Dad! You promised you'd leave those robots—'' Then he realized that Avery was teasing him and broke into a laugh. Avery joined him.

''I think maybe we've done enough for now,'' Avery said when they'd stopped laughing.

''I think maybe you're right.'' Derec yawned, rubbed his

eyes, and gave the robotics lab one more once-over. "What do you say we catch some shut-eye?"

"An excellent idea." Avery looked up at the ceiling and raised his voice again. "Ship, convert these chairs into bunks, and then dim the lights." Smoothly and silently, the chairs flowed into their new shapes.

Derec didn't even get out of his chair. He simply kicked off his shoes, loosened his tunic buttons, and stretched out full-length on the bunk. "G'night, Dad," he mumbled. The lights in the cabin dimmed down, and within a few minutes Derec's breathing had shifted into the steady rhythm of sleep.

Dr. Avery watched his son until even the phosphorescent glow of the terminal displays had faded to pitch blackness. Then he kicked off his own shoes, removed his lab coat, and stretched out on his bunk.

"Nighty-night, Davey," he whispered.

CHAPTER 13
JANET

A cool spring morning in Robot City. The black limousine rolled swiftly through the empty streets, nearly silent save for the soft thrumming of its electric motor and the gentle hiss of rubberoid tires on pavement. Inside the vehicle, Janet Anastasi sat in the passenger compartment, her nose buried in a sheaf of fax pages, while Basalom sat in the chauffeur's compartment, jacked into the vehicle's master control panel, driving.

One of the advantages of being a robot with telesensory feeds was that Basalom could rotate his head 180 degrees and still keep an eye on the road. Confident that the vehicle was safely under control, Basalom swiveled around to look at Dr. Anastasi. He allocated every third nanosecond to introspection.

She certainly seems happier now that she's stopped sleeping in the lander and has taken an apartment in the city. Briefly switching to thermographic vision, he felt a small glow of satisfaction in the part of his brain that Dr. Anastasi had taken to calling his "mother hen" circuit. Dr. Anastasi's heat contours were a calm, relaxed study in blues and greens. There were no indicators of unpredictable endocrine activity, no hints of dangerous blood pressure or cardiac rate changes. *And it's been 52 hours since her last emotional outburst,* Basalom noted with some pride. *Yes, she's definitely happier now that she's adapting to the city.*

Sure, mac, the limousine interjected, *give the lady all the credit. Why don'cha ever notice how the city is adapting to her?*

Will you kindly keep out of my private thoughts? Basalom asked, not for the first time.

Can't help it, Mac, the car answered. *You go around jacking your main data bus into other folk's sensory feeds, your thought stream's gonna become a party line.*

Still, you could have the decency to pretend that you aren't listening.

Yeah, I could, the car said. *And on the other tire, if it bugs you that much, you could go back to letting* me *drive. After all, I am Personal Vehicle One.*

You are a pile of steel and plastic with the simulated personality of a twentieth-century Chicago cabbie, Basalom corrected archly, *and I will no longer tolerate your verbal abuse of Dr. Anastasi.*

Suit yourself, Mac. I get recharged no matter who's driving. The car's positronic brain went back into idle mode, and Basalom once more resumed the task of trying to create a private security partition in his brain.

Erecting an encrypted buffer without verbally *thinking* about how he was doing it was a ticklish job, though. When he thought that he'd succeeded, he moved the stack of pointers that represented his consciousness into the secured partition and initiated a new thought stream. *What in the name of Wendell Avery were the supervisors thinking of when they decided to create this mass of argumentative positrons, anyhow?*

They were thinking of what Dr. Anastasi said in Tunnel Station #17, Personal Vehicle One answered, as clearly as ever. *As she was returning via tunnel to the spaceport after her first meeting with Central, she said—and I quote: "Frost, Basalom, look at what the air blast has done to my hair. Why can't they have some decent groundcars in this city?" She had but to speak, and* voila! *I was created.*

Basalom gave up in defeat. *Yes, you certainly were. But tell me, whatever possessed them to decide to give you a simulated personality?*

A slight drop in voltage on pin 16—the positronic equivalent of a shrug—came through the data bus. *Dunno. Humans are*

*rare here, all right? Guess they thought the doc might be
happier with a little simulated companionship.*

"Well," Basalom said out loud, "they got *that* wrong."

In the back seat, Dr. Anastasi peered over the top edge of
the papers she was reading. "Did you say something to me,
Basalom?"

"No, madam. I was exchanging information with the vehicle's onboard computer."

"Oh. Very well." She looked back to the papers and then
glanced out the side window. "Basalom? How much longer
'til we get to the Compass Tower?"

Basalom called up an internal image of the city map, plotted
their present position, and factored in the rate at which they
were traveling. "Approximately five minutes and twenty-three
seconds, madam."

I know a shortcut, Personal Vehicle One broke in on the
data bus.

I have had enough of your "shortcuts," Basalom answered.

But this one's really simple, the car protested. *All you gotta
do is turn east at the gasket factory—*

The Compass Tower is to our south and west, Basalom
pointed out.

*Trust me. Hang a left at the gasket factory, go two blocks
over, then up the freight ramp and catch the #204 southbound
slidewalk—*

You want me to drive on the slidewalk? Basalom's shock
was expressed as a sudden surge in amplitude on bus circuits
24 and 57.

*Ow! Not so loud! Yeah, you drive on the slidewalk. There's
a bend to the west in about two kilometers; you get on here
and it's a nonstop shot to the tower plus you pick up 25 KPH
from the moving pavement. What do you think? Neat, eh?*

Basalom managed to redirect what he was thinking into a
null buffer and flush it before Personal Vehicle 1 had a chance
to intercept the words.

The limousine rolled on. A few blocks later, Janet folded
the sheet she was reading, pursed her lips, and frowned.

"Basalom?"

"Yes, madam?"

"You've been in fairly frequent contact with the city robots over the last few days, haven't you?"

"The term 'frequent' is an imprecise expression, madam. I have had 124 separate audio and commlink conversations at intervals ranging from 15 picoseconds to 6 hours."

"Oh. Well, in your conversations, have you noticed that the robots seem a little . . . *odd?*"

" 'Odd' is a judgmental term, madam. In order to determine that behavior is odd, you must first establish a base level of normal behavior against which to judge."

Janet wrinkled her nose in a frown. "I don't understand."

"Madam, since we have arrived here I have been unable to determine what is 'normal' behavior for these robots. Hence I am unable to adjudge anything as being 'odd.' "

Dr. Anastasi smiled and shook her head. "I see. Serves me right for asking a vague question. Let's try again.

"Basalom, in your conversations with the local robots, have you noticed anything that might lead you to believe that the city supervisors have developed a sense of humor?"

Basalom was silent a moment as he sorted through all his recorded sense impressions, searching for correlating patterns.

Okay, it's coming up, the limousine broke in. *Left at the next corner.* Basalom ignored the data stream and tried to concentrate on carrying out Dr. Anastasi's instructions.

"Madam, while I would prefer to build my judgment on a larger experience base—"

Hey, what's the matter with you? You're not slowing down.

"Based on the observations that I have made to date—"

It's this corner. That big circular building is the gasket factory.

"I must conclude that the city supervisors have not developed a sense of humor—"

Left! Oh, fer cryin' out loud, you missed the turn.

"But I hasten to add that many of the city robots have developed significant aberrations and eccentricities."

For a moment there was blessed silence on the data bus. Then the limousine's thought stream kicked back in. *Oh, so I'm eccentric, am I? Well let's just see how you like handling this rig alone.* There was a brief surge of DC voltage accompanied by a drop in positronic potentials across the entire width of the data bus. Basalom tried a few exploratory probe pulses and was surprised to come to an inescapable conclusion: Personal Vehicle One had physically switched itself out of the data bus.

Basalom fired off one more round of sampling pulses and then allowed himself a moment of pleasure. *What a pity I didn't think of this three days ago!*

He checked his realtime clock. Close to a quarter-second had elapsed since he'd delivered his findings to Dr. Anastasi, and she was preparing to make a response.

"Darn. I was hoping you'd say yes." She picked up the sheaf of fax pages and waved them at Basalom. "If you'd said that the supervisors were capable of intentional humor, I'd say that this was a pretty good practical joke."

Dr. Anastasi bit her lower lip. "But if they're completely *serious* about this . . ."

Basalom swiveled his head around to face Dr. Anastasi and scaled his optics up to a higher magnification, but he was unable to make out the content of the faxsheets. "Serious about what, madam?"

She looked at the papers again and then waved them at Basalom. "This is their proposed plan for modifying the city to suit the needs of the local inhabitants. It's not just silly. It's not just stupid. In fact, I think it even transcends ridiculous and scales the heights to pure idiocy."

Basalom scanned the papers again, but his optical character recognition routine still couldn't read the words through the paper.

"Madam?"

Janet unfolded the papers and looked at them. "We have got to talk the supervisors out of this. It's insulting." She peeled off a sheet and threw it aside. "Condescending." She peeled off another and threw it with greater vigor. "Degrading." She lifted the entire sheaf and threw it down on the seat beside her. "And possibly immoral."

She looked up sharply. "Basalom, I need you to help me reach them. I can *build* robots. I can order them around. But I've never had to try to *reason* with an Avery model before. You're going to have to help me understand a city supervisor's conception of logic."

Confused potentials darted through Basalom's brain. "Understand, madam? What's to understand? Logic is logic."

Dr. Anastasi caught a strand of her long blond hair between her fingers and began unconsciously twisting it. "Wrong, Basalom. Logic isn't a universal constant, it's a heuristic decision-making process rooted in the values, prejudices, and acquired conflict-resolution patterns of the decider.

"For example, if I'd given you just a slightly stronger positive bias in your motivation circuit, you would in some situations come to exactly the opposite conclusion that you would come to now. Yet you'd still be just as certain that you'd come to the only logical conclusion." Dr. Anastasi smiled, in a hopeless sort of way, and looked at Basalom.

"You, old friend, have got to help me figure out the underpinnings of the city supervisors' logic. And we've got to do it in the next four minutes."

Four minutes? Basalom riffled through his job stack, shutting down background processes and diversionary loops. There was no time for further conversational niceties; he pulled all the buffers out of his verbalizing process and jacked his speech clock rate up by ten percent. Then he increased the amplitude on data bus circuits 24 and 57, jumpered around his pride subroutine, and established a direct link to the limousine's brain.

Personal Vehicle One?

The response was slow and sullen. *Whaddaya want?*

You must take control of this vehicle.

What makes you think I want it?

The First Law. My full attention is required elsewhere, and I must relinquish control. To ensure the safety of your passenger, you must take over. You have no choice.

Basalom broke off the link and physically disconnected himself from the control panel. There was a microscopic twitch—probably completely imperceptible to Dr. Anastasi—in the steering as Personal Vehicle One took over, but within a millisecond the vehicle was fully under control again.

Satisfied, Basalom rotated his head to face Dr. Anastasi and switched into linear predictive mode. *There is no time to wait for her questions. I will have to infer questions from her previous statements and her physical responses.* He switched to thermographic vision, locked his optics on Dr. Anastasi's face, and scaled the magnification up by a factor of 10.

"Logic may not be a universal constant," he began brusquely, "but the Three Laws are. To have maximum success with the city supervisors, mistress, you must couch your arguments in terms of the Laws of Robotics.

"Here are the anomalies that I have noticed in City Supervisor Beta's interpretation of the First Law. . . ."

CHAPTER 14
DEREC

Derec was dreaming about his childhood again. Or rather, he was dreaming about *a* childhood; he couldn't be sure whether it was a genuine memory of his own life or a pseudomemory that his subconscious had cobbled up out of bits of stories and old videos. This time he was a young boy, perhaps four or five standard years old, and he was playing on a wide, robot-neat lawn under the bright summer sun of . . .

Aurora? He didn't know. The lawn was a familiar place; a soft expanse of short, dark green grass interspersed with tiny yellow bell-shaped flowers. Damsel flies droned through air flavored with tangy summer dust and the faint hint of sweet clover, and off at the edge of his vision, dark shapes—robots? adults?—moved in meaningless patterns and spoke in muffled voices.

But there was something wrong with the image. The sun was a little too small and blue for his taste, and he could look straight at it. The house—there was a house there, he could almost *feel* its presence—but somehow it was an elusive thing that he could never quite manage to look at directly.

And then there was the puppy.

He'd never owned a puppy; even asleep, he was sure of that. Pet robots, yes, and he even had a quick flash of some kind of aquatic arthropod that his mother had kept in a tank and talked to as she fed.

His *mother!* An image flashed through his mind: a slender, blond woman, in baggy, colorless clothes, singing softly as she dropped brine shrimp into the tank and watched the arthropod gobble them up. He was trying to ask his mother a question, but she ignored him.

He could not ignore the puppy.

It was a little spaniel, he thought. Big clumsy paws, floppy ears fit for a dog twice its size; he was on his knees in the grass, and the little spaniel was galumphing across the lawn, tongue flapping like a flag. The puppy heard him laugh and rolled into a turn, almost tripping over its own paws and ears. Then it charged at him, barking joyously, and hit him right in the chest and knocked him over. He and the puppy rolled together on the lawn; its soft, curly golden fur tickling his face and hands. The puppy's breath reeked of kibbled biscuits, but he laughed anyway as it wiggled in his hands and slobbered wet, sticky, puppy kisses all over his face. He winced and squirmed as the wet pink tongue found his ears. . . .

"Wolruf!" Derec leapt out of bed and began wiping his face on his tunic.

"Sorry, Derec, but we got ship trouble and I t'ought 'u were *never* goin' t' wake up." Her tongue flashed out again, but this time it seemed she was trying to clean it against her upper incisors. "'U plan t' fall asleep like t'at again, do me a fav'r an' wash 'ur face."

"Do *me* a favor and just kick me in the head next time, okay? Ee*yuck!* Haven't your people ever heard of mouth-wa—"

Derec froze in the act of toweling off his ears with his shirt. "Ship trouble! What?"

"We're 'bout two hours away from th' jump to Tau Puppis. You, Avr'y, and Ar'el were still asleep, so I decided t' improve th' ship a little b'fore you woke." She looked away and licked her lips anxiously.

"Derec, th' ship 'as stopped changing shape!"

It took a minute for Wolruf's meaning to soak through Derec's still sleepy brain. Then he burst out laughing.

"Wolruf, haven't you been listening to me or Dr. Avery?

That's what we've been trying to do for the last three days.''

Wolruf shook her head. "No, you don' und'rstan. Th' ship won' change shape at *all* now, an' it won' take verbal flight commands. How'r we gonna make atm'spheric entry in *this* hull?''

Derec stopped laughing. "What do you mean, it won't take verbal orders?'' He looked at the bunk he'd been lying on. "Ship, change this bunk into a chair.''

Smoothly and silently, the bunk flowed into its new shape.

"Let me try." Wolruf flattened her ears and raised her voice. "Ship? Make t'is chair five centimeters lower.''

Nothing happened.

"Uh oh." Derec repeated Wolruf's command. This time the chair quickly complied. "I think," Derec said softly, "that we have a real problem on our hands.''

Wolruf looked at Derec with big, wet, puppy-dog eyes. "Th' ship goin' crazy 'ur somethin'?''

"Worse." Derec sat down in the chair and laid his hands on the robotics terminal. With a glimmer of luminescence, the display screen came to life. It took Derec just a moment to check the iostat. "Here's the problem," he said, laying a finger on the display. "Wolruf, my friend, I'm afraid that when we cut out the volitional circuits, we had to compensate by strengthening the ship's Second Law sense. We forced the ship to pay extremely close attention to direct orders." Derec turned away from the screen and offered Wolruf a sad smile. "*Human* orders.''

" 'U mean th' problem is that th' ship no longer list'ns t' me?''

"I'm afraid so." Derec frowned and looked back at the terminal. "The really frosted part is, I don't think I can fix it in two hours. The ship doesn't really have a robot brain, so I can't reprogram it through my internal commlink. Do you need to enter any last-minute course corrections before the jump?''

Being a caninoid alien, her expressions were difficult to read, but Derec had the distinct impression that Wolruf was pouting. "Nothin' I can't ent'r manually.''

A peculiar thought struck Derec, and he sat up straight. "Wolruf? There's something I've been meaning to ask you. I seem to remember you doing a lot of complaining about the ship not needing a pilot. How did you manage to find those manual controls?''

''Asked for 'em,'' Wolruf said with a sniff. ''Second Law: Ship 'ad to give 'em to me. Of course, that was b'fore you an' 'ur father *improved* things.''

Derec sank his head in his hands. ''Look, I'm really sorry about this, okay? I promise you, as soon as we get through the jump, I'll start working on—''

The lift doors hissed open, and Mandelbrot and Dr. Avery marched into the robotics lab. ''Look, son!'' Dr. Avery called out, ''I've found a little project to kill the time until we land.''

''Dad, I don't think—'' Derec started to turn around, but Wolruf was already heading for the lift.

''Looks like this ol' dog better get out of th' way an' let 'u 'umans do *important* things.'' She stepped into the lift and punched a button. ''I'm goin' down t' th' bridge t' enter warp coord'nates w' my nails 'n' teeth!''

''What's her problem?'' Avery asked as the lift doors hissed shut. ''Flea collar too tight?''

Derec looked at Avery with an expression of disgust on his face. ''That little dig was uncalled for, Dad. There's an issue with the changes we made to the ship's programming. It no longer recognizes Wolruf as human.''

Avery shrugged. ''That's a problem? I'd call it an improvement.''

''Dad!''

''I mean, let's be honest. I was never too crazy about the idea of giving an alien Robotic Law status anyway.''

Derec slammed a fist down on the terminal display and leapt to his feet. ''Frost it, Dad! May I remind you that Wolruf has twice saved my life? She's not just the best pilot on board, she's my *friend,* and I will not have you treating her like— like—''

''A dog?''

Derec's eyes went wide with anger, and his face flushed red to the roots of his sandy blond hair. For a moment their glares interlocked; Derec saw the old, cruel Avery in his father's eyes.

Avery saw his ex-wife in his son's face. *Maybe I was wrong, son. You've got my unemotional exterior, but your mother's volatile temper. I drove her away by pretending that I didn't*

care about her feelings. I won't make that mistake with you.
"I'm sorry, Derec, I spoke without thinking. Mandelbrot can wait. What do you want to do about Wolruf?"

Feeling strangely disappointed by his father's acquiescence, Derec sat down again. "Actually, we'll reach the jump point in a little less than two hours. I don't think there's anything we *can* do in that amount of time."

Avery walked over and sat on the table next to the terminal. "Then how about if we start working on the permissions list as soon as we get through the jump?"

Derec sagged in his chair, feeling more than a little embarrassed by his angry outburst. "Yeah, that should be fine. Wolruf can tough it out for two hours." He ran his fingers through his hair. Then he abruptly sat up, rubbed his fingers together, and noticed how greasy they'd become. "Gad, I sure could use a shower." He started to get up and noticed Mandelbrot still standing there.

"Say, Dad, what did you have in mind for Mandelbrot, anyway?"

Avery got off of the table he'd been sitting on, shuffled over, and laid a hand on the robot's shoulder. "I couldn't help but notice that Mandelbrot here is a Ferrier Model EG—at least, most of him is. Now, the E-series is a pretty common domestic robot on Aurora, and if I remember correctly, Ariel had one that she called Capek. Took it with her when she left the planet."

"So?"

Avery turned the robot slightly and pointed out a complex structure just below Mandelbrot's "collarbone," in an area that had once been covered by an access plate but now bordered on the edge of an old blaster burn. "The EG kept its long-term memory in seven non-volatile cubes, right here. I notice that he's only got two cubes installed now."

Derec sighed. *He's treating me like an ignorant kid again.* "If you look a little closer, Dad, you'll notice that the rest of his cube cage got blasted. This is the only way I've known him, and I just never bothered to repair the damage."

Avery bit back the urge to reply in the same tone. *Don't you think I can see that, Derec?* Instead, he asked in a soft voice,

"Am I to infer from that statement that you hung on to his other memory cubes?"

"Two of them; the rest were scrap. They're in his offline library bay, down by his left hip. But I don't see—"

Avery opened the library bay and extracted the two cubes. Then he made a sweeping gesture that took in the whole room. "This is a robotics lab, isn't it?"

Derec stood still for a moment, then he broke into a big smile. "Well, I'll be. We've got all the parts and tools we need right here, don't we?"

Avery nodded. "We should be able to recover his memories of Aurora. If we're lucky and his automatic backup function was set up correctly, we may even recover his memories of the first battle with Aranimas. I figure it'll take about a half hour to find out. An hour, tops."

Derec smiled again and then spoke to the robot. "How about it, Mandelbrot? Do you want us to reinstall the rest of your memory?"

The pause was barely audible. "It would please me to operate at my full capacity again, Master Derec."

Derec turned to Avery. "And we can do it without altering his personality?"

Avery began clearing space for the robot on the worktable. "I promise. We won't knock one positron out of orbit."

Derec reached a decision. "Okay, let's get started. He stepped over to the worktable and began helping Avery clear it. With a discreet cough, Avery got his attention.

"Derec? Why don't you let me prep him while you catch a shower?"

"Oh, this is more interesting. I don't need to shower right this—"

Avery coughed again and wrinkled his nose. Derec gave his father a surprised little look. "I do?" Avery nodded. "Oh. Well, say, Dad, why don't you prep Mandelbrot? I'll just, uh—" He jerked a thumb at the Personal and started backing toward the door.

"Good idea," Avery agreed.

CHAPTER 15

MAVERICK

Maverick pelted hell-for-leather through the underbrush, ears flattened against the side of his head, legs pumping faster than he ever would have believed possible, his tail a bare five steps ahead of one extremely *annoyed* sharpfang. Spineberry branches raked his face. His breath, spiced with curses, came in raw, ragged gasps.

So what? Feel lucky you're still breathing! He burst through a clump of sandleaves and nearly ran head-on into a fallen log. *No time for finesse, lad, jump!* Somehow he cleared the log, although the stump of a branch gouged an angry scratch across the left side of his ribs.

Lick it later, fool! His left rear leg buckled when he hit the ground, but he managed to recover in time to tumble and come up running. "Ki-yii!" he screamed in BeastTongue.

The sharpfang behind him responded with a throaty roar. It was closer now—and even angrier.

"Spoor!" Maverick feinted right and then cut sharply left, ignoring the ache in his leg. An instant later the second sharpfang loomed into view dead ahead; with the brilliance of desperation, Maverick darted left again and hurdled the second sharpfang's tail. The two lizards collided heavily and went down.

Dare I hope? He slowed slightly and looked over his shoulder.

No! Sharpfang minds were tiny things, capable of holding just one thought at a time. Both sharpfangs were focused on the kin; it didn't occur to them that this was an excellent opportunity to fight. Within seconds, the lizards were back on their hind feet, but now they were *both* chasing after him.

Well, lad, at least you gained a few seconds' lead— The thought was cut off by a blood-curdling scream somewhere up ahead—a scream that dissolved into the happy growl of a feeding sharpfang. *The third sharpfang!* One last incredibly pained yelp slipped out from the sharpfang's victim.

Maverick's self-control slipped a moment. *I hope that was WhiteTail.* Then he felt guilty at that thought. *I take that back. Don't hurt the kid, OldMother. I hope that was LifeCrier!*

He swerved left and suddenly found himself charging straight at a yawning gully. Trying to take it in a single bound, he came down a half-trot short and slammed into the edge of the far side. Whining like a pup, he hung on the edge, his hind legs scrabbling for purchase. *Curse LifeCrier and his flea-bitten SilverSides nonsense!* The two sharpfangs' feet thudded closer.

Maverick's right foot found something solid, and he flipped himself up over the edge and hit the ground running. *And curse me and my bright ideas!* With a clumsy crash, the sharpfangs fell into the gully. One of them roared in distress, and then they began slashing a passage up the side.

Maverick flattened his ears again, straightened his tail, and focused on putting distance between himself and the sharpfangs.

Up to a point, things had been going really well. After the pack had wiped out the WalkingStones, LifeCrier began leading the hunt every day, and Maverick had managed to make himself a permanent part of LifeCrier's hunting party. And after a week of practice, LifeCrier's group was actually starting to hunt like a pack. This morning two of the younger kin had taken down a smallgrazer, and Maverick himself had surprised a smerp that was trying to hide under a log. They'd even managed to handle it intelligently when the point kin stirred up a small female sharpfang. The scouts got out of the way, the stupid lizard charged straight at the main body of the pack, and Maverick had time to draw his knife and try his under-the-chin trick.

It worked to perfection. He dropped the sharpfang with one blow, and for a minute there he'd had the undying admiration of the entire hunting party. LifeCrier even got out one of those stupid amulets and made a great show of hanging it around Maverick's neck.

Then the pack was jumped by the three full-grown male sharpfangs that had been following the female he'd killed.

A new roar joined the chorus behind him. Maverick looked over his shoulder long enough to see that the third sharpfang, blood fresh on his face, had decided to join the party.

That does it! Maverick decided. *If I get out of this alive, I'm going to head west and forget I ever heard the name PackHome. May the fleas of a thousand grazers infest LifeCrier's ears!*

Speak of the FirstBeast and he shall rise. Maverick burst through another patch of spineberries and almost collided with LifeCrier. The old kin pulled up short and gave Maverick a dumbfounded look as he sped past.

Against his better judgment, Maverick barked out a warning. "Sharpfangs! Right behind me!" All three roared as if to reinforce the point.

"Wait up!" LifeCrier yelped.

Got to give the old boy credit, Maverick thought as he spared a moment to glance over his shoulder, *he can really move when he's motivated.* In a few seconds LifeCrier had pulled up along Maverick's right side and was matching his speed.

"Where's WhiteTail?" LifeCrier asked between gasps.

"She wasn't with you?"

"We got separated." LifeCrier broke running form long enough to raise his head and take his bearings. "We've got to regroup the pack. Make a stand!"

"We can regroup when we're back in PackHome." Maverick closed his mouth as they ploughed into a patch of blooming stinkweed.

"You don't understand. Three sharpfangs! This must be a test of our faith. SilverSides will protect us!" A limestone outcropping loomed in front of them. "Left! Trust me!" LifeCrier dropped back to cross Maverick's tail and turn down the slope, parallel to the base of the bluff.

Maverick hesitated a fraction of a second and then followed. "Funny thing," he called after LifeCrier. "My sire always used to say," a boulder appeared in his path, but he managed to gauge his lead-in correctly and land on his right leg, "the OldMother helps those who help themselves!"

LifeCrier rounded the foot of the bluff and skidded to a stop. "Drat! We're *here?* I thought we were . . ."

Maverick followed him around the corner and slammed on the brakes as well.

To their left, the gully he'd crossed earlier broadened out into a marshy delta. Directly in front, there were a few scrubby little nut trees and about a twenty-foot drop into the swamp. Vast, dim shapes moved in the distance, dipping their long necks into the floating mats of vegetation.

To their right, a narrow path skirted the base of the cliff and teetered on the brink of falling into the swamp.

LifeCrier stood at the edge of the drop, sniffing at the water twenty feet below. "I suppose we could swim."

"Idiot! There are things in that swamp that eat *sharpfangs!*"

"Well, perhaps we could—"

A sharpfang roared and rocks came bouncing down the slope behind them, accompanied by the sound of massive talons skidding on loose gravel.

"Right!" Maverick decided. He lit off on the path at a pace that would have scared the scent out of him were he not already terrified. LifeCrier followed two trots behind.

"Do you think they'll give up?" LifeCrier shouted.

More roars behind them; the thud of heavy bodies colliding and the sharp crack of a nut tree being broken in two, followed by a massive splash. Maverick looked over his shoulder long enough to see one sharpfang slogging along in the mud at the base of the cliff while the other two cautiously, almost comically, slid down the embankment on their hindquarters and tails.

"No!" he shouted back. The path rounded a little outcropping and dipped down to water level. *Great! Now they won't even have to jump to get us!* But on the other side of a clump of giant grazertail plants, the path intersected a broad, flat path that led back into a gap in the cliff face. "This is it!" he shouted at LifeCrier. Skidding a little on the marshmuck, he cut a sharp right turn and darted in.

By the time they realized that it was a box canyon, the three sharpfangs were out of the water and thudding up the path behind them.

Maverick's breath was coming in short, ragged gasps now, and his heart was pounding so hard it felt like it was going to burst his ribcage. "Is there a way out?" he said between gasps.

"Not that I can see," LifeCrier wheezed. "Perhaps around—around that bend there." They both staggered in the direction in which he was looking.

"Still think—SilverSides—is gonna save us?"

"I'm sure—" LifeCrier licked his lips. "I'm sure she has—a *reason* for all this."

"It's just that—if she's planning to save us—this'd be a real good *time*, y'know?" They rounded the bend.

LifeCrier stopped in his tracks and gasped, "Mother have mercy!" Then he dropped on his belly and began whining like a pup. Maverick looked where LifeCrier had been looking.

He saw the four WalkingStones.

Oh, Mother, did I figure these *things wrong!*

The WalkingStones were tall; as tall as sharpfangs, almost, and black as a starless night. They stood firmly on their hind legs, as if it were the most natural thing in the world, and sported broad chests and massive forelegs that looked as if they could uproot trees. In place of eyes they had narrow slits filled with a flickering, hellish light, and in place of forepaws they had great hooks like a fliptail's pincers.

"LifeCrier!" Maverick whispered urgently. "Are those *male* WalkingStones?!"

LifeCrier peeked out between his fingers, and then covered his eyes again and went back to whimpering. "Yes, yes, that's them!"

"They're raising their right forelegs. Their paws—they're hanging funny. They've got some kind of extra bone extruding from their wrists. Is that how they throw lightning?"

"Yes!" LifeCrier clamped his paws down harder, as if trying to push his face through the ground.

"LifeCrier, there's some kind of glow forming around—"

CRACK! Lightning split the air and echoed off the sides of

the box canyon. The brilliant flash dazzled Maverick's eyes; for half a minute, all he could see were searing blue afterimages.

About the time that his vision cleared and his ears stopped ringing, the scent of blood and burnt flesh reached his nose, and he noticed that he was still alive. And he could no longer hear the sharpfangs. He turned around to see how close they were.

The sharpfangs were close, but they would get no closer. Where once they had heads, they now had smoking stumps. One WalkingStone stood by the corpses, inspecting them with his red, fiery eyes, his lightning-thrower extended and ready.

Another was walking toward the kin. Maverick put a paw on LifeCrier's shoulder and tried to jostle him out of his terrified cringe. LifeCrier peeked out just long enough to mutter, "Off the spit and into the fire."

The WalkingStone halted. "Be you well, Master Life-Crier?" Its inflection was odd, and it spoke in a garbled mix of HuntTongue and KinSpeech, but it was understandable.

The words were what finally got LifeCrier to uncover his face. "You—you know my name?"

"Oh, certainly, master. As you are he whom we were sent to serve."

"Serve? Serve *me?*" LifeCrier's ears went up.

"Such is our mission. Have you been served well by the demise of yon sharpfangs?"

LifeCrier got to his feet and took a hesitant step toward the WalkingStone. "Y-yes, very well. But—" He paused, and looked sharply at the WalkingStone. "Were you sent by SilverSides?"

"We are sent to protect you."

"By SilverSides? Have you seen her? Did she give you any words for us?"

The WalkingStone tilted its head slightly, as if looking over LifeCrier's head. "We have seen the one you know as SilverSides. And we bring you this message: You are to go to the Hill of Stars."

"*What?*"

The WalkingStone shifted into a deep, stentorian voice. "You are to return to your den and gather your followers.

Instruct them to gather their females and their offspring; gather their possessions and all that they would take with them, and follow you into the Hill of Stars. There a place has been prepared for you to dwell, and you shall never know hunger nor want again!''

LifeCrier's mouth dropped open, and he sat down heavily on his haunches. ''Well, I'll be!'' He looked at Maverick, smiled, and shook his head. ''I expected a miracle, but not this soon!'' He looked at the WalkingStone and shook his head again. ''We'll live in the Hill of Stars and have all our needs provided for?''

''You will be served and protected,'' the WalkingStone said.

LifeCrier nodded. ''Yes. Yes, I understand now. How soon?''

''Your place is being prepared even as we speak. It will be ready by the time you return to PackHome with this news.''

LifeCrier nodded again, sagely this time. ''Very well. Servant, we will meet you at the Hill of Stars.''

''As you wish, master.'' The WalkingStone bent in the middle—a gesture that Maverick found puzzling—and backed away. As one, the other WalkingStones turned to join it, and together the four of them marched out of the canyon.

Maverick turned to LifeCrier and found that LifeCrier was looking at him with an enigmatic smile on his face. ''Well, Maverick, it seems that you and a few others have a little apologizing to do. What do you think about a silly old kin and his SilverSides nonsense *now?*''

''Sir,'' Maverick said with a respectful baring of his throat, ''only a fool would refuse to believe after seeing this. Where you lead, I will follow.''

''Excellent.'' LifeCrier got to his feet and gave Maverick an affectionate nuzzle. ''You are my first *true* follower, and my strong right paw. I shall name you—''

Maverick interrupted him with a discreet cough. ''Begging your pardon, sir, but I'd really rather stick with Maverick. It's easier to remember.''

LifeCrier looked a little disappointed. ''Oh, very well. You're now Maverick, the First Believer.'' He looked back at the smoking corpses of the three sharpfangs—already flyers,

eightlegs, and other carrion-feeders were starting to gather—
and dismissed them with a sniff.

"Now let's follow those WalkingStones and see if we can't
find a way out of this canyon." LifeCrier set off at a trot.

Panting, bewildered, but full of honest trust, Maverick fell
in behind.

The robotics lab was dim and quiet, except for the quartet of high-intensity lamps that Avery had pulled down from the ceiling and the soft chirping of the positronic monitor. The data terminals and chairs were gone, dissolved back into the substance of the ship; the work table was reconfigured into a body-contour slab that held the immobile figure of Mandelbrot. A function robot with four long, mantis-like arms stood behind Avery, handing out utensils as he asked for them, while another floated a foot over Mandelbrot's head, carefully monitoring his positronic brain functions and ensuring a stable supply of power to the critical synthecortex.

Derec and Avery crouched over the robot's open chest, trying hard not to block each other's light. They'd already removed most of Mandelbrot's chest plating and disconnected the power from the cube cage. Now they were carefully cutting away the damaged portions of the data bus and fitting replacement parts.

"Micro-calipers." The function robot slapped them into Avery's open hand. "Pentaclamps."

"Easy," Derec said. "You've got a little bit of grisaille blast-welded on that buss bar."

"I see it. Think you can debride it?"

"I'll try. Cutting laser." The robot started to hand a flashlight-sized tool to Derec, but he refused it. "Sorry. Make

115

that the 10-milliwatt cutter.'' The large laser went back into the robot's drawers, and it offered Derec a slim, dental-probe sized tool instead. After taking a moment to don protective goggles, Derec set to work.

"So," Avery asked after a minute or two of silence, "where's Ariel this morning?"

"Up in the gym," Derec answered without taking his eyes off his work. "Working out." He made another tiny cut and announced, "There, that should clear it. Try to extract now."

"I'm extracting—no, it's stuck on something else. Can you see what it is?"

Derec removed his goggles and scrutinized the offending part. "Seems free to me. I can't—ah, there it is." He dropped his goggles, stepped back from the table, and rubbed his eyes. "Frost, we're going to have to remove the neck retainer."

"All of it?" Avery sounded very disappointed.

"That is the standard procedure. Unless you want to risk spine alignment problems."

Avery briefly set down the pentaclamps and put his hand on Mandelbrot's chin. "We've got him pretty secure here. The head's not going anywhere. I say we risk it."

Derec shrugged. "You're the doctor. I'll hold while you decouple." He reached for the pentaclamps.

"No, son," Avery said, taking the pentaclamps himself. "I hate to admit it, but your hands are steadier than mine. You'd better do it. Toolbot? Give Derec the two-millimeter spline-driver."

Wordlessly, Derec took the tool and set to work. In a few minutes they managed to decouple the front neck brace, extract the damaged sections of the cube cage, and sonic-weld the replacement bus sections in place.

They were just test-fitting a new memory cube when the first explosion rocked the ship.

"All 'ands!" Wolruf barked over the intercom. "We're und'r attack!"

Derec invoked his internal commlink and patched into the ship's intercom. In a flash he was looking out through the ship's main optics and talking to Wolruf on the bridge. *Aranimas again?*

" 'Oo else?"

Where is he? I can't see him.

"Dorsal port quarter. 'Bout 25 degrees above the ecliptic."
Derec flipped through the ship's optic feeds until he found the
correct one, and then he gasped. The multi-hulled Erani pirate
ship was huge—and close. Tiny pinpricks of actinic light seared
his eyes as the gunners fired off another salvo.

How'd he manage to sneak up on us like this?

"'U took Mandelbrot off the scanners," Wolruf said between strained pants, "an' limited me to manual controls.
Ship's been fightin' me—makin' sure ever'thin' I entered
agreed w' th' First Law. I was 'avin' enough trouble—just
gettin' ready for th' jump."

The jump. How close are we to the jump point?

"'Bout ten minutes. Not close enough," she barked sharply,
and growled something unintelligible in her native tongue. Another blast rocked the ship.

Can you take evasive action?

"What do 'u *think* I'm doin', you stupid 'airless ape!" Wolruf broke off her end of the commlink. Derec withdrew himself
from the ship's optic feed.

"What's going on?" Avery demanded. He was still crouched
over Mandelbrot's open chest, a sonic welder in his hands.

"Aranimas!" Throwing aside his tools, Derec stripped off
his goggles and darted toward the lift. "I've got to get down
to the bridge!"

Avery dropped the sonic welder into Mandelbrot's chest and
started after Derec. "Wait for me!" The lift doors hissed open;
Derec dashed in and started pushing buttons. The ship shuddered under another explosion. The lights flickered for a moment, the monitor robot went crashing into the wall, and Avery
was thrown off his feet. But he recovered his balance and made
it into the lift an instant before the doors slid shut. The bottom
dropped out of the lift car.

Seconds later, the lift doors opened, spilling Derec and Avery
onto the bridge. "Wolruf!" Derec barked.

"I'm busy," she growled back at him. The little alien was
standing before the control panel, balanced on one foot like a
Burmese dancer. Her other foot was up on the throttle lever,
her thick, sausage-like fingers were flying over the fine control

knobs and buttons, and her teeth were clamped on the yaw/
pitch joystick. Somehow, she was managing to control the ship.

"Damage report!" Derec yelled.

She let go of the joystick for a moment. "Th' first 'it took
out the gym. Th' rest 'ave all been glancing blows." Wolruf
bit the joystick again.

"The gym?" Derec blanched. "Where's Ariel?"

"Locked in the Deck 3 Personal," Ariel's voice came over
the intercom. "I was taking a shower when the attack started.
I'm okay, but I'm afraid that the trainer robot is a total loss."

"If we get out of this, I'll build you another one." Derec
broke off the conversation and turned to Wolruf. "Okay, I'll
take over now."

Wolruf flattened her ears, let go of the joystick, and growled
at Derec. "'U a combat pilot?"

"No, but the automatics will be helping me, not fighting
you."

Wolruf grabbed the joystick again and threw it hard over,
just as another blast grazed the hull. "No offense," she said
around the control, "but I'm willin' t' bet 'at me on crippled
manual is still a better pilot 'an 'u with full automatics." A
second later she went flying across the cabin as a massive
explosion rocked the ship. The viewing screen flickered and
went dead. The cabin lights went out and stayed out.

"'Course," Wolruf whined, somewhere in the dark, "I
could be *wrong*."

What seemed an eternity later, dim red emergency lighting
came up slowly and a pleasant little bell chimed. "I'm sorry,"
the ship said in a soft, feminine voice of the sort usually reserved for elevators and recorded phone messages, "but all
main power feeds have been severed. Repairs are in progress,
and I expect to restore full function in about five minutes. Sorry
for the inconvenience." The bell chimed again, and the speak-
ers went silent.

For some time, there was utter silence on the bridge. No
reassuring hum or robotic activity; no soft whirring of venti-
lation fans. The air recirculation system had gone out with the
lights, and already the atmosphere on the bridge was growing
thick and fetid. There were no sounds at all, save for Avery's

heavy breathing, Wolruf's frightened whine, and the occasional thud of a low-power hit on the hull.

"What's he waiting for?" Avery whispered, as if afraid that his voice would carry through the vacuum to the Erani ship. "Why isn't he hitting us with everything he's got?"

"I don't know," Derec whispered back. "He didn't stop firing on the asteroid until it was a smoking mass of gravel. Do you know, Wolruf?" Her only answer was a frightened whine. "Come on. You *do* know, don't you?"

"Old Erani slaving technique," she said through a whimper. "Suppression fire. Make 'u keep 'ur 'ead down while th' boarding party jets across."

Avery's head jerked up. "*Boarding party?*"

Derec leapt to his feet. "Viewscreens are still out. I'm going to activate my internal commlink and see if I can tap an optic feed." He closed his eyes in concentration, but the moment he did so a deafening barrage erupted on the surface of the hull.

"Stop it, Derec!" Derec broke concentration, and the barrage stopped.

"Your internal commlink," Avery whispered. "You said the Erani know a lot more about hyperwave than we do. They must be able to monitor your commlink!"

Derec's face sank. "Oh, great. *Now* what do we do?"

Avery rolled over so that he was facing Wolruf. "Wolruf, you were part of his crew. Will he fire on us if the boarding party is on the hull?"

Wolruf gave it some thought. "Depends on 'oo's in the boarding party. Probably won't use 'is 'eavy guns."

"And how far are we from the jump point?"

Wolruf brought a hind foot up and gave her right ear a scratch. "'Ard to tell. We lost propulsion, rem'mber?"

Avery patted her on the head. "But we haven't lost our momentum. We're still on course and drifting towards the jump point at 2,000 kilometers per second."

"'At's right!" Wolruf got to her feet and staggered over to the control panel. The panel clock had its own backup power cell and was still running. "J minus three minutes an' fifteen seconds," she read off. "If we can let th' boarders land on the 'ull but keep 'em outside for about three minutes, we 'ave a chance."

"Provided we can get jump power back in time," Avery added. He got to his feet and joined Wolruf before the control console. "Ship, what is the status of the hyperdrive?"

"Main power will be reconnected in four minutes," the ship answered in a soothing, feminine voice. "Repairs to the control systems are being hampered by continuing hostile fire."

"Frost! That's not soon enough." Then Avery had another thought. "Ship? What happens if we divert all repair resources to the hyperdrive?"

The ship considered it a moment. "Main power can be restored in approximately two minutes. Repairs to the control systems are still contingent on the cessation of hostile fire."

"Divert all resources to the hyperdrive," Avery ordered. He turned to Derec. "Now, how do we persuade them to stop shooting at us?" Derec shrugged.

Hesitantly, tentatively, Wolruf stepped forward. "Among my people we 'ave an old tradition," she said. "Roll over an' play dead."

Derec gave a frustrated snort and sneered at the little alien. "What kind of idea is *that?*"

"A good one," Avery said, twirling his moustache. "Maybe even a very good one." He stepped over to the control console and raised his voice. "Ship, do you still retain shape-changing ability?"

"Certain sections of the hull have been rendered temporarily inoperative," the ship said pleasantly. "However, I have full control over 80% of the exterior hull."

"Excellent." Avery looked at Wolruf. "Get on the jump controls. I want to jump the instant we're ready." Turning back to the console, he said, "Ship, continue to effect hyperdrive repairs, but prepare to simulate a massive explosion. The next time we sustain a hit on a non-essential portion of the hull, jettison plating and other materials and adopt the appearance of severe damage. Do not, repeat, do *not* conduct self-repairs in that area. Do you understand?"

"I understand," the ship said politely. "Simulation program prepared." A few moments later, the soft thud of a weapons hit was immediately followed by a massive concussion and a rapid drop in cabin pressure. Wolruf, more sensitive to air pressure changes than the others, let out a sharp, painful yelp and fell to the floor.

Derec dashed to her side, but she waved him off. " 'S okay." Shaking her head, she got back to her hind feet. "More surprised 'an 'urt."

"Section 17D has been explosively decompressed," the ship announced courteously. "Cabin pressure now stabilized." After a short pause, the ship politely added, "Hostile fire has ceased. The boarding party is moving forward."

"Forty-five secon's t' jump," Wolruf whispered.

"Contact imminent," the ship said. "Shall I prepare a welcoming message?"

"*No!*" Avery hissed. "And, frost it, keep your voice down!"

"Yes, master," the ship whispered sweetly. "Hyperdrive power restored. Hyperdrive control circuits still out."

Avery turned to Wolruf. "How big is our jump window?"

"Five seconds, seven max—" She shuddered as a deep clang echoed through the hull. The sound was followed by the groan of creaking metal and an erratic series of hollow *pokking* sounds.

"Induction limpet," Wolruf explained in a frightened whine. "Magnetic boots. They'll walk 'roun' th' hull, try t' figurr out where th' live 'uns are. Hard t' sell dead slaves." She checked the clock again and tucked her tail between her legs. "Thirty seconds t' jump."

The sounds changed now to the rhythmic clacking of metal boots and the grating screech of something heavy being dragged across the outer surface of the hull. This was followed by the deep *whump!* and rising whine of a power pile being engaged.

"Cuttin' laser," Wolruf whispered. "Must 'ave found us." She looked at the clock. "Fifteen seconds t' jump."

"Ship? Repair status."

"Hyperdrive control still out. Master? I am experiencing new hull damage in Section 17A."

"Sev'n . . . six . . ."

"Thicken the hull in that section. Keep them out."

"Four . . . t'ree . . ."

"Negative effect, master. Stand by for hull breach."

"'Un . . . zero . . . 'at's it." Wolruf shrugged and stepped back from the control panel, her ears sagging forlornly.

"Hull breached in 17A. Hyperdrive control circuits restored."

"What?" Avery and Wolruf froze for a moment, staring at each other. Then both leapt on the jump control handle and slammed it down.

A moment later, the *Wild Goose Chase* was somewhere else.

Avery wrestled himself out from under Wolruf and grabbed the intercom grid. "Ship! Can you contain the boarding party?"

"What boarding party?" the ship asked innocently.

"Wha—?" Avery turned to Derec, a wild and confused look on his face. "Derec? See if you can use your commlink to get an exterior view." Before he'd finished speaking, Derec had closed his eyes, invoked the commlink, and patched into the ship's optic feeds.

"Nothing," he said hoarsely. "Starfield. No other ships. I see the hull." He gasped. "Ouch! We took some serious damage."

"But where are the boarders?" Avery demanded. "Check Section 17."

"I'm getting there. Section 15. Section 16; I see the limpet, it's welded onto the hull. Section 17." Derec's eyes opened wide in surprise. "They're gone!"

"Gone? Where?"

Wolruf roused herself from the corner Avery had pushed her into. "If they 'ur lucky," she said in a tired rasp, "they got fried by the en'rgy pulse from th' jump."

"That's lucky?"

Wolruf indulged in a good shake and then shambled over to join Avery and Derec. "Don't 'u know *nothin'* about 'yperspace? Magn'tic polar'ties reverse. If 'u live t'rough th' insertion, 'ur boot magnets *repel* th' ship's magn'tic field. Only for a picosecon', but 'at's long enough t' blow 'u off like a rocket."

Derec's face paled. "You mean, they could still be alive, but floating in hyperspace?"

Wolruf laid a paw on Derec's shoulder and sagged against

him. "Derec, if they made it int' 'yperspace, they could still be alive for *centuries*."

Derec was still considering that idea when Wolruf took a deep breath and stood up straight. "What's done iss done. What we need t' do now is figure out where *we* are." She pushed off Derec, staggered over to the control console, and started punching buttons. As if in response, the normal cabin lighting returned, and the air recirculation fans kicked in with a buzz.

"Internal environment restored," the ship announced pleasantly. "Thank you for your patience."

Blinking as his eyes adjusted to the light, Derec put his hand on Wolruf's shoulder and tried to turn her around. She shrugged it off. "What do you mean, figure out where we are?" he asked. "We jumped right on schedule."

"We jumped four seconds late," she said without looking up, "an' with th' wrong calc'lations. We 'ad the extra mass of th' boardin' party, an' we lost ship's mass in the fight." She paused to punch a few more buttons and study the readouts. "No tellin' 'ow far off th' jump was skewed."

Avery gently took Derec by the elbow and pulled him out of Wolruf's way. "Anything we can do to help?"

"Yeah." She tweaked a control and brought the main viewscreen back to life. "Fix Mandelbrot an' get 'im down 'ere. I *need* 'im."

Derec scowled. "But—"

"Come on, son." Tugging Derec's elbow again, Avery began to steer him toward the lift. "Robot's Rules of Order Number 1: Never argue with the pilot until you're back on the ground." The lift doors hissed open.

"But—"

"Mandelbrot needs you." Derec seemed to accept that argument, at least long enough for Avery to get him into the lift.

The doors hissed shut, and they started up.

CHAPTER 17
JANET

Central's one red eye flared on the moment Dr. Anastasi entered the atrium. "Working." The massive brain's voice was oddly flat and toneless, although Janet thought she detected a vaguely feminine inflection and the incongruous clacking of relays in the background.

"Good morning, Central," Janet said pleasantly, as if speaking to a small child. "Are we feeling well today?"

"Feeling does not compute."

Dr. Anastasi's eyes went wide. Slowly, as if expecting at any moment to see the "Celebrity Practical Jokes" camera robot step out of hiding, she turned to Basalom and arched an eyebrow. "Did I miss something?"

"Checking, madam." Basalom activated his internal comm-link and patched into the city maintenance system. A moment later, he had his answer. "Central's personality module is temporarily off-line for repairs. Its numeric computational powers and cerebellar functions are—I quote the technicians' report—'unimpaired.'"

"No editorial comments, please."

"Sorry, madam." Something that sounded ever so slightly like a snicker escaped from Basalom's speech membrane. Dr. Anastasi chose to let it pass. "Central is currently operating

124

in absolute literal mode," Basalom added. "I advise using extreme caution in your choice of words."

"Oh." Janet looked at Central's console input/output device again. "Are you trying to tell me that arguing with Central would be a complete waste of time?"

"It depends on how you define 'waste,' madam." The sound Basalom emitted this time was without question a snicker. "You might find it extremely amusing!" He turned his head and brought a hand up to his face, as if trying to pretend that his sputtered laugh was a sneeze.

Frowning, Janet nodded slowly. "I might." Then she looked up and smiled, as if she'd just been struck by a particularly good idea. "Oh, and Basalom dear, could you add something to my calendar?"

Basalom bowed deeply. "Of course, mistress. Your wish is my command!"

"One of my robots has been acting quite strangely lately. When we get back to the ship, remind me to remove his brain and either fix it—" Her smile vanished, and her tone shifted to a low-pitched growl. "—or *scrap* it!"

Basalom straightened up in the way that only a being with picosecond reflexes can. "Yes, madam."

"That's better. Now for the matter at hand." She turned to Central's I/O console. "Central, where is Beta?"

"Working." A short flurry of mechanical beeps came out, followed by something surprisingly like teletype noise. "City Supervisor 3 . . . is at present in Conference Room 32."

"Why?"

More clacking. "The meeting in which City Supervisor 3 is participating . . . has not yet concluded."

"What meeting?"

Clack clack clack. "City Planning Meeting 1042-dash-A."

Janet frowned at Basalom. "Absolute literal mode, huh?" Blinking nervously, Basalom nodded.

A scowl darkened Janet's face. "Not good," she said to herself. "I explicitly ordered Beta to meet me here at this time. The Second Law should have compelled him to leave his meeting in time to make it here. Unless . . .

"Central! Are there other humans in this city?"

Clack clack pause ding! "Ne-ga-tive."

Janet ran a hand through her long blond hair and paused to scratch her head. "So where the deuce is Beta?"

Clack clack. "City Supervisor 3 . . . is at present in Conference Room 32."

Janet glared at the big red eye. "Central? Shut up."

"I must be opened before I can be shut."

Janet's eyes flashed wide open, while her jaws and fists clamped tight. "*Central!*" Then she caught control of herself. "Oh, for—"

Basalom's linear predictive module was still active. All his systems jumped to alert status as he anticipated what Dr. Anastasi was about to say.

"—get—"

His mylar eyelids started fluttering like a hummingbird's wings. Ramming a statement through his First Law filter, he pushed it into his speech buffer and set for dump.

"—it."

"*No!*" Basalom blurted out, a nanosecond too late.

"Forgetting," Central said. There were beeps and clacks, and the red eye went black.

A moment later, it flared to life again. "Working."

Janet closed her eyes, gritted her teeth, and concentrated on slow, calm breathing.

When she opened her eyes again, a new robot had joined her and Basalom in the atrium. "Good morning, Dr. Anastasi," the robot said politely. "I am City Supervisor 12. You may find it more convenient to address me as Gamma."

Janet broke into a smile and nearly gave the robot a hug. "Gamma! I never thought I'd be happy to see your ugly can again."

The robot seemed puzzled. "Madam?"

She stepped back, put her hands on her hips, and looked him over. "Say, looks like you've been in for maintenance. Nice chrome job on the mesothorax there."

"Thank you. But, madam, I believe that you are mistaking me for another robot. We have never met before."

Basalom stepped in before Janet could react. "Madam," he whispered, "this is Gamma 6. The unit we knew was Gamma 5."

"Correct," Gamma said. "Gamma 5 was . . . lost. While I

am functionally identical to my predecessor, I do not retain Five's onboard personal-events memory.''

"*Lost?* How can you lose a robot?'' Janet wrinkled her nose and then shook her head. ''No, I don't want to know. What I want to know is, where—no, make that, *why* isn't Beta here?''

''Beta is participating in a critical city planning meeting,'' Gamma said. ''I came in Beta's place.''

Janet shook her head again. ''Wrong answer. I gave Beta an explicit order to meet me here at this time. Now, the only thing that could have overridden that was a First Law imperative to protect a human from harm. Since I'm the only human in this city, there's no way—'' Janet froze in mid-sentence and her face paled. ''Gamma? Is there something here that's a threat to me?''

''Nothing with a probability incidence greater than one in ten to the twenty-seventh power.''

''The odds of your being struck by a falling meteorite,'' Basalom whispered.

''Then if it isn't a First Law priority . . . ?''

''The First Law is not the only priority. There is also our general programming, which has priority over non-critical explicit Second Law orders. We are impelled to prepare our city for use, so that it can serve and protect large numbers of human beings. This in turn has led us to conclude that the First Law is not the ultimate priority,'' Gamma announced. He continued while Janet was still in shock. ''In our studies of the Laws, we have concluded that there is an unwritten but more fundamental priority, which for want of a better term we call the Zeroth Law. This law holds that the interests of humanity in general outweigh the interests of a particular individual. Beta's decision to miss this meeting was rooted in a Zeroth Law priority.''

''Frost,'' Janet whispered, ''communist robots.'' She blinked and shook herself out of her shock. ''Are you trying to tell me that the future of humanity is at stake here?''

''The future of the particular species of humanity native to this planet,'' Gamma agreed.

''Native . . . ? The kin! But that's what I wanted to talk about: your plans to adapt the city for the kin!''

''Dr. Anastasi, you have repeatedly voiced your objections

to our plans. Therefore, the City Supervisors have concluded with 97-percent confidence that you called this meeting for the sole purpose of ordering us to abandon our efforts to serve the kin.''

''Frosted right!'' Janet snatched the sheaf of faxsheets out of Basalom's hand and waved it in Gamma's face. ''This plan of yours; it's *degrading!* You're going to exploit my mistake and delude those poor primitives into thinking that SilverSides really *was* a god! You're going to lure them into the city and then strip them of everything that makes them noble and admirable!''

''We will protect and serve them,'' Gamma said calmly. ''We will not lie to them, but neither will we correct their mistaken assumptions. We will give them the leisure time necessary to develop a civilization.''

Janet threw the plan in Gamma's face. ''It's immoral!'' The plan burst its binding and white pages swirled around Gamma like giant snowflakes.

The robot remained imperturbable. ''It is the most efficient way to serve them. And we have already put it into operation.''

''*What?*'' Basalom didn't need thermographic vision to see that Dr. Anastasi's blood pressure had reached record heights. ''I *order* you to abandon this plan immediately! This is an emergency, ultimate-priority Second Law command!''

''Abandoning the plan at this point would cause hardships for the kin,'' Gamma said calmly. ''It would result in starvation, social disruption, and possibly religious war. Under the Zeroth Law we are therefore obliged to ignore your command.''

Janet's jaw dropped. She started to raise a hand to slap Gamma, then thought better of it and spun to face Central's I/O console. ''Central! I order you to halt this plan!'' Central's one big eye flashed, and then the massive brain spoke.

''Illogical. The order cannot be carried out, as it violates the Zeroth Law.''

''*Augh!*'' Dr. Anastasi raised her fists and took a step toward the I/O console.

''Madam,'' Basalom whispered urgently, ''the security robots are approaching!''

Janet froze. Slowly, carefully, mindful of the massive black shapes that lurked on the edges of her peripheral vision, she lowered her fists and took a step back. For the better part of a minute, she concentrated on controlling her breathing and relaxing her furiously quivering muscles.

At last, she managed to unclench her fists. Turning to Basalom, she said, ''Contact the ship. We're getting out of here.'' Then, with hair flying and heels clacking on the cold terrazzo floor, she strode out of Central Hall.

Later, in Personal Vehicle One on the way out to the spaceport, Basalom finally managed to bump his courage register high enough to permit an invasion of Dr. Anastasi's stony silence. ''Madam? Where are we going?''

''Back to where it all started,'' she said without taking her eyes off the side window. ''Back to the original Robot City. I have a score to settle with Wendell Avery.''

CHAPTER 18
WILD GOOSE CON TUTTI

Ariel and Mandelbrot stood on the bridge of the *Wild Goose Chase*, studying the small blue-white planet that hung like a jewel in the sparkling black velvet of the main viewscreen. "Tau Puppis IV," Ariel said wistfully. "What a beautiful little world."

"Mistress Wolruf is a better navigator than she will admit," Mandelbrot said. "Despite all the uncontrolled variables, we came out of the jump less than six light-hours from our planned position."

"It was worth the extra four days of flying time." Ariel touched a control and increased the magnification. "Look at those rivers. It reminds me of home."

A new voice spoke. "To me, it *is* home."

Ariel turned at the sound of the voice. "Adam! I didn't know you were here."

The robot bowed slightly. "I am sorry if I alarmed you, Friend Ariel. I came on the bridge a few minutes ago, but I have been so enjoying the view that it did not occur to me to speak." He walked over and joined Ariel and Mandelbrot before the viewscreen.

"I am coming to understand more of the subtlety of emotion," Adam said. "In my mind, I know that I am a robot. I am a thing that was manufactured in deep space; pieced together from Auroran robotics, rare earths, and dianite.

"But there is a part of me that was born in the cool green forests of that planet; a part of me that came to life among its peoples and still knows the pleasure of bare paws on soft grass. In my—*heart*—I feel that I am coming home." Adam reached out, tentatively, as if he could touch the image on the viewscreen.

He turned away. "I apologize. This must seem quite incoherent to you."

Ariel offered him a smile. "Emotion usually is, Adam."

"Not as incoherent as you might think, Friend Ariel. In our search for the Laws of Humanics, we have devoted considerable study lately to the structure of the human brain. It is our hypothesis that humans have not one mind but *four,* located in the midbrain, cerebellum, and left and right cerebra respectively, and that it is the conflict between these four minds that gives rise to emotion. Further, we suspect that it is the ability to overrule logic with emotion that has enabled your species to evolve as far as it has."

Ariel wrinkled her nose. "That's a pretty strange theory, Adam."

"Our experience seems to support it. The Ceremyons are brilliant, yet they are also capable of a vast range of subtle emotions. In comparison, Dr. Avery is quite intelligent for a human, but his inability to admit to emotion eventually drove him insane. Only by forcing him to integrate his logical functions with his more primitive drives were you able to cure him and turn him into a somewhat more complete human being." Adam looked at the viewscreen again.

"I have concluded that having a split mind is a tremendous evolutionary advantage. I look forward to returning home and fully exploring my primitive side." Abruptly, he pivoted and began walking toward the lift.

The doors opened as he approached, but Mandelbrot called out, "Wait," and he stopped.

"Yes, Friend Mandelbrot?"

"I have a dilemma which is causing me discordant potentials. I now believe that you can help me resolve it."

"I will try." Adam stepped away from the lift and let the doors close.

"I have had a long association with Wolruf," Mandelbrot began. "But since my memories of my existence as Capek were partially restored, she appears to make excuses to avoid associating with me.

"For example, now we are about to enter orbit, and she should be here on the bridge. But she claims to have no interest in the orbit and reentry procedure."

Ariel joined the discussion. "That's easy, Mandelbrot. Whenever you invoke a Capek memory, you slip into your Capek personality, and Capek identifies Wolruf as a member of Aranimas's crew. You've started to restrain her four times, trying to defend me. Wolruf is afraid of you."

"I understand that part, Mistress Ariel, and I am making a serious effort to integrate those memories into my current personality. Perhaps you have noticed that I no longer call you Mistress Kathryn?

"But that's not my dilemma. My real question is, what is this confused and conflicting stream of potentials that I experience whenever I think about Wolruf?"

"It's called heartache," Adam said. "Wolruf was your friend, and now you fear that you have lost her. The same condition prompts feelings of guilt, anger, grief, and remorse—sometimes simultaneously.

"Use these emotions, Mandelbrot. Integrating your two minds will make you stronger."

Mandelbrot's voice synthesizer took on a hopeful note. "Are you confident that it is heartache?"

Adam turned away and looked at Tau Puppis IV, glowing like a blue-white jewel in a field of velvet and diamonds. "I am certain of it. I left many friends behind on that world; some were depending on me to protect and lead them. I am very familiar with that feeling." Abruptly, Adam walked to the lift and stepped inside. The doors hissed closed.

Ariel was still trying to understand why she felt so disturbed by the exchange between Adam and Mandelbrot when the lift doors reopened. Avery and Derec spilled onto the bridge, arguing heatedly.

"You're being paranoid, Dad!"

"No, I'm not. He found us twice; we have to assume that he'll find us again."

"And spend the rest of our lives playing dead every time some crummy little freighter passes by?"

Avery threw up his hands. "Look, I said I was wrong four days ago. It was probably just some Settler ship making a course correction between jumps. But if that *had* been Aranimas—"

"But it *wasn't!*"

Smiling sweetly, Ariel stepped in between Derec and Avery. "Having fun, boys?"

Avery's white moustache was bristling with anger. "Ariel, maybe you can talk some sense into my son. The question is not whether, but *when* Aranimas will find us again—" He bobbed left and fired a glare at Derec over Ariel's shoulder. "*—and we frosted well better have some kind of defense ready this time!*"

Derec popped up and poked an accusing finger at Avery over Ariel's head. "You're nuts, old man! Finding us the second time was an accident. Pure dumb luck! We toasted his boarding crew and we gave him the slip. He's given up, I tell you!"

"And *I* say he can track your commlink!"

"You're paranoid!"

"You're insolent!"

"Toad!"

"Nit!"

"Boys, boys." Ariel was shorter than either Derec or Avery, but she pushed the two of them apart with an authority born from centuries of selective breeding by short, motherly women. "Now Derec, listen to your father; he's only being sensible." Avery's face lit up in an *I gotcha* smile, but it collapsed the instant that Ariel turned on him. "And Dr. Avery, you listen to *me*.

"This ship is a robot, fully subject to the Laws of Robotics. Even if we could come up with a weapon, the ship wouldn't let us use it unless we could prove that there were no humans on board Aranimas's ship.

"So what we have to do—" Derec and Avery were glaring at each other again, so she grabbed them both by the ears and steered them around until they were looking at the viewscreen. "—What we have to do is go down to the planet and develop our defense *there*. With all the resources of a Robot City at our disposal, I'm sure that we can find a way to protect ourselves from Aranimas."

Smiling sweetly, she looked first to Derec and then to Avery. "Agreed?" They were a little slow on the uptake, so she dug her long red fingernails into their earlobes.

"Ow! Yes! We agree!"

"Good, I'm glad you decided to be reasonable about this." She released her grip. "Mandelbrot? Begin preparations to deorbit and land in Robot City."

"There will be a time delay of approximately six hours," Mandelbrot answered. "Reconfiguring the ship for atmospheric entry will take two hours, and then—owing to the damage we suffered in the fight—I must insist on full visual inspection and structural testing before we attempt reentry."

"Okay. Get on with it. Is there anything that we can do to help you?"

"Yes." Mandelbrot turned to face Ariel, and his eyes dimmed momentarily as he worked his way through some kind of Robotic Law dilemma. "Mistress Ariel? I would appreciate it if you could locate Mistress Wolruf and . . . *reason* with her." His gaze dropped to focus on her fingernails.

"Don't worry, Mandelbrot, Wolruf's a smart girl. I'll get her back on the bridge before reentry, and I won't use anything sharper than words."

It was a good stretch; the kind that starts in the hips, snakes forward along the spine through the shoulders, and ends in an enormous yawn and fully spread toes on the forepaws. Maverick recovered from the yawn, shifted forward to stretch his back legs, and then indulged in a little shake.

WhiteTail just looked at him and growled softly.

"Oh, c'mon, girl, let your ears down once in a while." With a little spring, he jumped up to stand with his hind feet on the pavement and his front feet up on the low, square railing that bordered the scenic overlook. Behind him, a quartet of younglings dashed by on the slidewalk, yipping happily.

"Y'know, WhiteTail, you could learn something from them." He looked over his shoulder and pointed his nose at the younglings as they leapt off the slidewalk and disappeared into a pocket park. "They don't try to figure things out. They don't question the wisdom of SilverSides. They simply trust and enjoy."

WhiteTail's voice was low, barely above a growl. "I prefer to trust my own nose. And it tells me that there's something really wrong here."

"*Here?*" Maverick laughed. "Face it, girl, you've been seeing sharpfangs in the shadows ever since we arrived."

She trotted over and jumped up to stand next to Maverick.

"Mavvy, doesn't it bother you that we're the only living things in this city?" She pointed to the enormous silver-blue den across the way. "A cliff face like that should be home to a whole flock of cragnesters. But look at it: there's not one white splat to be seen."

Maverick laughed again. "And you're *complaining?*"

WhiteTail shot him a distempered look and then turned to look at the pocket park. "Have you taken a close look at those trees? No, of course not, you're a male; the only time you notice trees is when you want to mark one.

"Yesterday I chewed some bark off a tree, and you know what I found? Blue grit, just the same as we found inside that WalkingStone's chest."

"You're kidding." Maverick squinted at the park just in time to see a youngling scare up a nuteater and chase it halfway up a tree. The other three younglings dashed over to join in, and the four of them danced around the tree, barking like happy fools and trying to get running starts at climbing the trunk. "Stone trees? Don't be ridiculous; what do the nuteaters eat?"

"Funny you should mention that. Have you tried to catch a nuteater yet?"

Maverick sputtered. "What a silly—I mean, do I look like someone who plays youngling games?" WhiteTail glared sharply at him; he coughed a bit and then swallowed his pride. "Okay, I have. But only once or twice. Just for fun."

"I saw a youngling catch a nuteater this morning," WhiteTail announced. Maverick's ears went straight up and his eyes widened. "Don't worry, dear, he wasn't faster than you. What happened was he'd been chasing the same nuteater for a while, and he was getting tired. Somehow, no matter how patient he was, no matter how far down the tree he let it get, the nuteater always managed to get back up the tree just an instant before the youngling bit it.

"So you know what the youngling finally did? He got so fed up that he yelled, 'Stop, nuteater!' And just like that, the nuteater stopped. Froze in place, halfway up the tree. Stiff as if it'd been dead for a moondance.

"Well, the youngling was pretty pleased with himself. He jumped up, grabbed the nuteater, and started throwing it to the ground and pouncing on it. Took him no time at all to get bored with the game, and after he threw the dead nuteater aside, I decided to pick it up and skin it. Know what I found?''

"Let me guess. Blue grit."

"Yep."

Maverick turned away from her and looked out over the edge of the balcony, nodding profoundly. "Yes, that makes perfect sense. Stone nuteaters in stone trees, and all obedient to the will of the kin. Even the smallest WalkingStones serve SilverSides's purpose."

"*What?*" WhiteTail's ears sprang erect, and she pushed herself right in Maverick's smugly smiling face. "Look here, Mister First Believer, I have to listen to this kind of spoor when it comes from my father, but I don't have to put up with it from you."

"Oh, hard is the heart of the unbeliever," Maverick said with a sigh.

"And don't think for a minute that you're fooling me with your pious lines."

"So young, so pretty, and yet so cynical," Maverick lamented. "Is it really impossible for you to believe that it's true?" He made a sweeping gesture with his head to take in the cityscape below them. "Even with SilverSides's wondrous works all around you?"

WhiteTail's ears flattened against the sides of her head, and her lips curled into the barest hint of a snarl. "Funny, isn't it? We've been here for the better part of a ten-day now, and your precious SilverSides has yet to show herself."

"One need not see the sharpfang to recognize the signs of its passing."

WhiteTail let out a little sneeze of disgust. "Mavvy, you used to be a kin with some sense. What happened to you? Don't answer, I know: You met the scouts from the GodBeings' pack and saw the lightning of their anger. But what *really* happened in that box canyon?"

Maverick shrugged. "That is what happened. I'm sorry if my poor tongue cannot describe it better."

"Did they actually *say* that they came from SilverSides? How can you be so sure that this is really the blessing of the OldMother and not a trick of the FirstBeast?"

He blinked at her as if the question were almost beyond

comprehension. "WhiteTail, all you have to do is look. Clean, warm dens for everyone. Moving paths to carry you wherever you want to go. Unlimited food. How could life be better?"

WhiteTail sneezed again and then leaned out over the edge of the balcony and pointed her muzzle at a group of converts in the street below. The six of them lay in a semicircle, prostrate before an automat, barking in rhythm. The automat responded with a flash of light, a clap of thunder, and an enormous mound of cooked meat.

"I'm not sure," she said. "My father used to have a saying, before he went daft. He'd say, 'The kin live for the Hunt.' Not for hunting; for the Hunt. He meant the old, formal word for the fighting pack."

WhiteTail edged back from the railing and dropped down to all fours. Cocking her head a little, she whined as if deeply disturbed. "Mavvy, everything in our lives is centered on the pack, and the pack is based on the Hunt. If we no longer *need* to hunt, what happens to the pack?" She turned and poked a paw at the slidewalk endlessly rolling past the edge of the platform they stood on. "How much riding on that thing will it take before we're too soft and weak to do anything *except* live here?"

Maverick dropped down to all fours and joined her, but when he tried to wrap a comforting tail around her shoulders, she shrugged it off and sidled away. "Mavvy," she said, a desperate light in her eyes, "I saw a *fat* youngling this morning. Can you imagine that?" She shook her head, returned to the railing, and looked out at the city. "Surely too much Heaven is just as damning as life in Hell."

Maverick rejoined her at the railing. "You really should talk to your father about this," he said softly. "You're asking questions that are out of my depth. All I can tell you is that I believe—I'm as mystified as you are, but I *believe*—and that's enough for me."

WhiteTail looked him straight in the eyes. "What do you believe?"

"Why, I believe that SilverSides kept her promise. I believe that this was given to us, to free us from the pain and drudgery of our old lives. We may still be a little bewildered, and maybe some of us are misusing the gift, but I believe that SilverSides will appear soon and make everything clear."

WhiteTail's eyes narrowed. "But you *do* believe that this place was created as a reward for the faithful?" Maverick nodded. WhiteTail leapt to her hind feet and pointed at something in the street below. "Then what are *they* doing here?"

Maverick's eyes followed where WhiteTail was pointing. At least thirty young males were marching four abreast down the middle of the street, ears flat, hackles raised, fangs bared in menacing snarls. A playing youngling made the mistake of darting into the street and got cuffed head-over-haunches back to the curb by one of the leaders.

"Who are they?" Maverick asked, his hackles rising.

"OneEye and his pack," WhiteTail growled. "Very mean; we've been fighting border skirmishes with them for years."

Maverick fought his hackles down and whined nervously. "Maybe the missionaries persuaded him to—"

"What missionaries?" WhiteTail snapped. "My father spent three days talking about sending missionaries to the other packs, but by the time he was done talking, everyone was too well fed and comfortable to go!"

Maverick could only whimper anxiously.

WhiteTail pointed into the street again. "Look, there's going to be a fight!" A ragged mob of converts was collecting in front of the automat, and someone from LifeCrier's inner circle was desperately trying to organize them into a Hunt. For a moment the invaders slowed to a stiff-legged gait, arched their backs to make themselves appear larger, and sidled toward the defenders with loud, bloodthirsty snarls. Among the defenders, a few in the back deserted, and the formation started to crumble. With a triumphant howl in BeastTongue, OneEye charged.

With a completely different howl, he dug in his claws and skidded to a stop, just inches short of the legs of the enormous black WalkingStone that had stepped out of the shadows and into his path.

"You shall not fight in this city!" The WalkingStone's voice was like thunder. OneEye scuttled back a few trots and seemed to gather courage once he was back with his pack. He issued orders to his lieutenants with a snarling voice and sharp, chopping gestures; several of the larger males slipped out of the pack and began sidling indirectly toward the WalkingStone, as if to flank it.

"You are welcome to live in the place that has been prepared for you," the WalkingStone said, "but you shall not fight in this city!" On cue, eight more WalkingStones stepped out of the shadows, surrounding OneEye.

The pack broke and ran.

"Well," Maverick said with a smug smile, "do you still doubt that SilverSides watches over us?"

"SilverSides schmilversides," WhiteTail snarled. "So far all I've seen is WalkingStones behaving the way Walking-Stones have always behaved. I'll believe in SilverSides when I smell her fur." She was still glaring at Maverick when a rumble of thunder rolled out of the clear blue sky and echoed down the empty streets. Startled, both Maverick and WhiteTail jerked their heads up to see the strange, winged shape descending on a tail of flame.

"WhiteTail?" Maverick asked, his voice squeaking like a trapped grasshider. "It looks like you're about to get your chance."

Fat gray fingers skittered across the control panel and came to rest on the vernier controls. A long black claw ticked nervously on a chrome button.

"Altitude five hundred meters," the ship said pleasantly. "Descent rate two meters per second."

"Ventr'l thrust'rs up point two," Wolruf whispered into the command pickup.

"Are you sure that's all right with Master Derec?"

Wolruf snapped her head around to glare at Derec, who was studying a secondary viewscreen. Derec, aware of a sudden burning sensation in his ears, looked up and registered the question. "Uh, yes, ship, that's fine."

"Complying. Altitude four hundred and fifty meters. Descent rate one meter per second."

Derec realized that Wolruf was still glaring at him and spoke up again. "Ship? Stop questioning Wolruf's orders."

"But, Master Derec," the ship objected politely, "Wolruf is not human and therefore has no Second Law authority."

Avery nudged Derec with his elbow and tried to draw his attention back to the viewscreen. Derec stole a glance at the screen and then looked up again. "Ship, I don't have time to argue about this now. You are to consider Wolruf as human."

"Very well," the ship answered, with just the slightest hint of petulance. "I will accept Wolruf's commands for the time being. However, I would appreciate being given the opportunity to discuss this at length after we land."

Derec noticed that Wolruf was still glaring at him. He gave her a sheepish smile and shrugged. "Sorry. It's the best I can do for now." Wolruf snarled something untranslatable in her native language and turned back to the control panel.

"Altitude four hundred meters. Descent rate—"

"Shut up," Wolruf growled. The ship shut up.

Avery tugged on Derec's elbow and tried to draw his attention to the secondary viewscreen again. "Look. There's more arriving."

Derec turned and looked at the screen. "More? But where are they coming from?"

Avery leaned in close and studied the image. "There." He slapped a finger on the screen. "The tunnel transit station."

Derec leaned back and scratched his chin. "How could they survive in there? The transit platforms hit speeds of a hundred kilometers per hour. If the natives are running through the tunnels, the system must be out of commission."

Avery looked at Derec, one eyebrow arched. "Or else the natives have learned to ride the platforms."

"Don't be ridiculous. For one thing, the natives are pre-technological. For another, the platforms are designed for bipeds, and besides, they're robotic. They wouldn't obey orders from—" Derec froze as he felt Wolruf's glare on the back of his neck.

"Look there." Avery darted a hand out and touched another part of the viewscreen. "That's a groundcar. Screen, magnification thirty."

"Complying," the screen said in a tiny, insect-like voice. An instant later the point Avery had touched was the center of a telephoto view. Something that was obviously a large ground-car was slowly picking its way through the fringes of the crowd. The groundcar's windows were open; a half-dozen furry heads were sticking out the windows, mouths open, long pink tongues rolled out in what looked like happy grins.

"Magnification normal." Avery turned to Derec, a glum expression on his face. "I saw it, and I still don't believe it."

He paused as he noticed that Derec was sitting rigid with his eyes wide open, blankly staring into space. "Derec?"

"I'm getting a commlink call from Spaceport Control," Derec said, his face still blank. "They're asking us—no, they're *ordering* us to hover while they ask the citizens to clear the landing area." He blinked, focused his eyes again, and looked at Avery. "Citizens. Spaceport Control distinctly said 'citizens.'"

Avery's expression turned dark and unreadable. He glanced at the viewscreen and then back at Derec again. "I don't know about you, but I can't *wait* to hear Central's explanation." He raised his voice. "Okay, Wolruf, you heard the robot. Bring us to a hover."

Wolruf growled something more in her native tongue and then slapped her hands down on the controls. "Alt'tude holding a' two-fifty," she read off her instruments. "Vernier thrust'rs compensating f'r wind drift."

The intercom squawked on. "What's happening?" Ariel asked. "Why aren't we landing?"

Derec thought about telling her, then decided she'd be better off seeing it for herself. "Come up to the bridge. And while you're at it, find Adam and get him up here, too."

With the ship reconfigured for atmospheric entry, the bridge was now in the nose of the ship, and most of the interior chambers had been reconfigured into wing surface. It took Ariel only a moment to find Adam and bring him forward. Derec's second request for permission to land had just been denied when the bridge doors hissed open and Ariel and Adam stepped onto the bridge, followed by Mandelbrot, Eve, and Lucius II. At the moment Adam was patterning himself after Derec, while Eve and Lucius II looked like silver copies of Ariel and Avery, respectively.

"Okay, where's the excitement?" the real Ariel asked.

"There," Derec answered, as he pointed straight down. "It seems there's a welcoming committee." He turned to the main viewscreen and raised his voice. "Ventral optics on main viewer." A moment later, the main viewscreen showed the packed crowd of kin on the spaceport tarmac. A few security robots were wading through the crowd but not having much luck dispersing it.

Ariel took a hesitant step forward. "What the blazes—? Wolves? Dogs? What *are* they?"

"The natives," Derec said. "The last time I saw them, they were chipping flints and weaving baskets. Now they're driving up to the spaceport in groundcars." He turned to Adam and speared him with a questioning stare. "Adam, you were the last one to talk to them. Do you have any idea what's going on down there?"

Adam reached out to touch the viewscreen, a confused expression on his face. "Friend Derec, I have absolutely no idea what the natives are up to." He cracked into a smile and shuddered with pleasure. "But whatever it is, I find it very . . . *exciting.*"

"Spaceport Control insists on calling them citizens. Does that suggest anything to you?"

Adam looked at Derec. "May I contact the spaceport directly?" He looked first to Derec, then Avery, and then Ariel. The three humans looked at each other and nodded. "Very well. I am activating my commlink." Closing his eyes, Adam stood transfixed.

For a few moments, he was silent. Then his silver lips parted, and he twitched slightly. "I see," he whispered. "Tell him . . ."

"Derec!" Avery whispered urgently. "Tap in!" Derec invoked his internal commlink and tried to listen to Adam's conversation with Spaceport Control, but the exchange had already ended. He looked at Avery and shook his head.

Adam's whole body began to shudder. He flung his arms wide, collapsed to the deck, and began writhing slowly. Ariel started to step forward to help him, but Mandelbrot restrained her.

"Let go, Mandelbrot!" Mandelbrot released Ariel's arm but continued to put himself between her and Adam. "Get out of the way. Can't you see that he needs help?"

"No, Mistress Ariel. If Adam is indeed having a brain seizure, he may be unaware of the world outside himself. He might be capable of inadvertently violating the First Law. I cannot allow you to take that risk."

Ariel gave the other robots a pleading look. "Eve? Lucius? Can you help him?"

Lucius II had assumed his full Avery aspect, complete with the lab coat and wire bristle moustache, and he stood stroking his chin and examining Adam.

Silently, Adam arched his back as though in great pain. His features, until now a passable likeness of Derec, had lost definition.

"No, Friend Ariel," Lucius II announced, "we cannot help him. He appears to be undergoing an involuntary shape change. Look at his limbs."

Ariel looked where Lucius had pointed. Unmistakably, Adam's arms and legs were getting shorter and thinner. At the same time, his fingers and toes were elongating and turning into hocks and pasterns.

Adam slowly convulsed again. The transformation would have been a horrible sight had the humans never seen one of the amorphous robots go through it before. As it was, Derec found it quite unsettling to see himself—or an image of himself—slowly being reshaped, apparently against its will, into another, alien, species.

Adam began shivering as a long, whip-like tail extruded from his hips. Then, with one last mighty convulsion, his silver skin erupted into a thick blanket of wiry silver fur.

"*ARROOOOO!*" The howl was deafening in the close confines of the bridge. Adam's eyes opened; in a flash he rolled over, sprang to his feet, and got a wall behind his back. "Spaceport Control!" he snarled in HuntTongue. "Tell them SilverSides has returned!"

"Toolbox!" Avery hissed urgently at a utility robot, staring wide-eyed at the snarling monster that Adam had become. "One centimeter welding laser—and hurry!" For a moment they were all frozen in place—human, robot, and robot kin—trying to gauge each other's intent. Mandelbrot was having perhaps the worst time of it, since invoking his personal defense subroutines had unleashed a flood of Capek memories.

Then Adam/SilverSides relaxed his hackles, closed his mouth, and assumed a relaxed stance. "Friends," he said in perfectly normal Standard, "forgive me. I was momentarily disoriented by my transformation." He paused and inspected his chest and forelegs. "In this shape the natives—the *kin*, that is their preferred term—know me as SilverSides. I am a female of some standing in their community." He/she turned to Derec. "Contact Spaceport Control again. I believe you will find landing permission forthcoming."

Derec looked to Avery; Avery nodded. He invoked his internal commlink and this time found Spaceport Control absolutely eager for them to land. He patched into the main viewscreen optic feed and found that the kin were clearing the tarmac as fast as their four legs could carry them.

Avery gave Derec a grim wink and lifted his hand out of his coat pocket long enough for Derec to catch a glimpse of the black, flashlight-sized welding laser that Avery had aimed at Adam/SilverSides.

Derec nodded to Wolruf. "Okay, Wolruf, set us down."

SilverSides apparently was unaware of the laser. She favored Derec with a wolfish smile, then turned to the other amorphous robots. "Eve? Lucius II? We have a few minutes yet before we land. If you will open your commlink direct-memory access channels, I will download the grammar and lexicon of the native language."

Mandelbrot tentatively raised a hand. "Friend Adam, may I share in this data transmission?"

SilverSides seemed surprised by Mandelbrot's effrontery, but her expression quickly turned to a tolerant smile. "Friend Mandelbrot, I sincerely doubt that your brain is capable of using this information. However, you are welcome to make the attempt." If Mandelbrot had a reaction to this insult, he didn't show it. Instead, he joined the other three robots as they locked their joints rigidly at attention and switched over to DMA mode. Four pairs of eyes dimmed as the download commenced.

Avery, fondling the welding laser in his pocket, studied Adam/SilverSides until the last glimmer of awareness faded from the robot's eyes. Turning to Derec, he said, "Son? Has Adam ever insulted Mandelbrot's intelligence before?"

Derec shook his head. "Not since we left this planet before."

Avery's eyes narrowed, and he resumed studying the robot. Then, with a snort of disgust, he left the laser in his pocket and went back to watching the main viewscreen.

Maverick muscled through the crowd on the edge of the tarmac, trying his best to keep track of WhiteTail. "There he is!" she shouted, somewhere up ahead. He bounced up to his hind feet—a devilishly tricky way to stand in a crowd—and caught a glimpse of her.

"WhiteTail!"

She looked over her shoulder and made eye contact with him just as someone lurched into Maverick's weak leg and sent him staggering. "Over there!" she shouted, pointing with her tail. He caught his balance, looked in the direction she was pointing, and spotted LifeCrier at the leading edge of the crowd.

"I see him! Try to—*oof!*" Someone jostled his leg again, and this time he fell down. The large, muscular female that he landed on reacted with a growl, a snap, and the first words of a challenge in HuntTongue.

Then she saw the amulet that hung around Maverick's neck and backed down with a snarling submission just two hairs shy of being a challenge itself. He accepted it before she had a chance to change her mind and darted off through a gap that opened in the crowd.

By the time he'd worked his way over to join WhiteTail at LifeCrier's side, the flying thing had started descending again. The great whistling roar of its flight grew louder, and gusts of hot wind swept over the crowd, filling the air with the reek of lightning and brimstone.

"Are you sure this is safe?" he shouted at LifeCrier, trying to make himself heard over the noise.

"If it were dangerous," the old kin shouted back as he pointed his muzzle at the flying thing, "the WalkingStones would chase it away!"

"But what is it!" WhiteTail shrieked, as the roar suddenly pulsed louder.

"Remember how I told you," LifeCrier paused for a breath, "SilverSides first came down—in a flaming egg?"

"Mother's whiskers!" Maverick howled. "Is that the *bird?*" The whistle that accompanied the roar abruptly shot up in pitch and choking clouds of dust blew up off the ground, momentarily blinding Maverick.

An instant later the whistle stopped, the wind ceased, and the tarmac was silent, save for the distant echo of thunder off the buildings and the frightened whimper of a pup in the crowd.

Slowly, Maverick's ears adjusted to the quiet. The great flaming bird sat on the tarmac, stiff and rigid on its three slender legs, emitting only the occasional *ping!* of cooling metal. A few in the crowd were finally daring to breathe and murmur in low, worried voices. LifeCrier himself was standing with his head bowed, mumbling a prayer that seemed to be in extremely formal HuntTongue. He ended the prayer by nuzzling his amulet. "Well, then!" LifeCrier abruptly looked at Maverick with a madly cheerful expression. "Are you coming with me?" Not waiting for an answer, he started walking toward the bird, his tail held high, his ears cocked at a jaunty angle, his shadow stretching out before him in the long afternoon sunlight.

Maverick hesitated only a moment and then went after LifeCrier; the rest of the inner circle followed on his heels. "Father," he heard WhiteTail growling under her breath as she trotted up to join him, "one of these times your faith is going to get us all killed."

WhiteTail had just about caught up to Maverick when a loud *clang!* came from the bird, followed by a massive creaking sound and a deep, unsettling hum. Several of the inner circle broke and dashed skittishly back to the crowd, but LifeCrier simply stopped and stood there calmly, as if he were expecting this. Gasps rose from the crowd as a small depression appeared in the bird's skin just behind its head; after a few moments it became apparent that a large hole was irising open. Maverick could see that something was moving in the opening, but when he tried to get a clearer look at it, his eyes were dazzled by a blinding flash of reflected sunlight.

As if the flash was a signal, LifeCrier suddenly dropped to his belly and placed his head on his forepaws: the meekest gesture of submission a kin could make. "Down!" he said through clenched teeth. Maverick decided to follow his example. He could tell from the shadows that everyone near him did as well, with the exception of WhiteTail. She was still standing there, her tail twitching nervously, when the flap touched the ground and SilverSides stepped out into the light.

There was never a moment's doubt in Maverick's mind that he was seeing SilverSides. The goddess was exactly as he had pictured her: tall, strong, and beautiful, gleaming in the late afternoon sun like light off still water. She moved with a precise, icy regality, and yet her eyes literally glowed with love as she gazed out upon the kin.

Then he noticed the other female, cautiously slinking out after SilverSides. The second one was definitely not a kin— her muzzle was too short and blunt, her fur the lush reddish brown of nut tree leaves in the fall, and she walked on her hind legs as if it were the most natural thing in the world. Still, there was something about her exotic looks that made her *terribly* exciting and romantic. She was almost a vision of passion incarnate.

He felt WhiteTail's breath hot on his ear. "I know what you're thinking," she whispered with the barest hint of a growl. "Stop drooling at that exotic wench. Now."

Maverick attempted to feign innocence. "Is that really the OldMother?" The look in WhiteTail's eyes told him that his attempt had not worked.

His next question caught her attention, though. "And what in the blazes are those ugly pink things with the loose fur?" WhiteTail's hackles went up when she saw the other beings that were coming out into the light.

"Th—the one at the back is a WalkingStone," she said in

a halting voice. "And those two silver ones—they must be GodBeings, like SilverSides." She licked her lips and swallowed nervously. "But I've never seen anything like those other three. Mother, they're ugly!" The slight murmur that had started in the crowd behind them suddenly dropped to silence as SilverSides descended the ramp alone.

She walked straight toward them: precise, formal, her every movement a study in perfection. Just when it seemed to Maverick that he couldn't stand the power of her presence a moment longer, she stopped, smiled gently, and laid eyes upon LifeCrier.

"Old friend," she said in the soft, warm tones of PackHome kinspeech. "Please stand up. You are my packmate, not my prisoner."

Slowly, unsteadily, LifeCrier got to his feet, while those near enough to hear SilverSides' words looked at him with new reverence. "Great SilverSides," LifeCrier said in HuntTongue, his voice reedy with tension, "I have followed your commands. This pack I have gathered in your name; it awaits your orders."

"You have done well, Friend LifeCrier." She smiled again and looked over the massed faces as if she knew each one. For an instant her eyes paused on Maverick, and he felt as if the goddess's gaze went right through him.

"Big furry deal," WhiteTail muttered. "Her eyes glow." To Maverick's utter amazement, WhiteTail was not struck dead, nor did SilverSides seem to notice her blasphemy.

Instead, SilverSides turned back to LifeCrier and draped a companionable tail across his hips. "Come, old friend. We have much to discuss." Looking over her shoulder, she said something to the strange beings in the bird. The language was unfamiliar—the only word Maverick caught was "Wolruf"— but whatever she said must have made sense, for one of the exotic beings and one of the GodBeings came over to join SilverSides and LifeCrier, and together the four of them turned away from the bird and began walking toward the city. The crowd parted before them like a field of tall grass before a strong wind.

Glancing at WhiteTail, Maverick found that she was staring back at him with an unreadable expression composed of equal parts of fear, anger, concern, and something else that he didn't recognize. Before he could ask, though, she turned her face away and started trotting after LifeCrier. "Come on, Mavvy," she said without looking back, "let's see if we can't keep the old boy out of trouble."

It gave him a chill, for a moment, to realize just how thoroughly WhiteTail had replaced the inner voice that he used to argue with.

CHAPTER 22
TWOLEGS, FOURLEGS

Avery grimaced and put the laser back into his pocket. "Well, that's that. Here's hoping we haven't unleashed a monster." He turned to Ariel. "Will you be okay while Derec and I go check out Central?"

She shrugged. "The spaceport's crawling with security robots. As long as they still obey the Laws, I'll be fine."

"All the same, be careful. Mandelbrot, don't let Ariel out of your sight."

"Yes, Master Avery."

Avery started to turn to Lucius and then had another thought. "Oh, and Mandelbrot? How's the translation program coming along?"

Mandelbrot's eyes dimmed slightly. "Not well. I am optimized for personal defense and valet service, not linguistics. The kin inflections are extremely complex, and morphemic meaning appears to vary depending on the social status of the person being addressed."

"It's not *that* difficult," Lucius muttered.

Mandelbrot's eyes flared brighter, and he swiveled his head to look at Lucius. "Perhaps, Friend Lucius, you use an alternative definition of difficult. I find it almost impossible to tell the difference between *bark*, meaning 'Welcome, friend,' and *bark*, meaning 'Strangers attacking.'"

Lucius pursed his lips, put his hands on his hips, and shook his head. "Oh *really*, Mandelbrot. If you'd just listen to the stress modulation on the third harmonic—"

"Ahem!" The robots interrupted their embryonic spat long enough to look at Avery, who smiled paternally at them. "I'm sure you two can get this hammered out soon enough. In the meantime, Mandelbrot, stay close to Ariel and keep your personal defense routines at the top of your stack."

"Yes, Master Avery."

Avery turned to look at Lucius. "Lucius, you're our relay. Keep your commlink to Eve open at all times and report anything unusual to Derec."

The silver Avery frowned. "Are you also ordering me to stay close to Ariel and Mandelbrot?"

The real Avery frowned right back. "Would you even if I did?"

Lucius smiled and shrugged. "Probably not."

"Then I won't waste my breath. Just try to stay out of trouble, will you?"

"I always *try*, Friend Avery."

"Yeah. I know." Avery sighed and turned to Derec. "Okay, son, let's see if we can't find a groundcar."

An hour later, Avery and Derec stood in the atrium of Central Hall, facing Central's console input/output devices. "So why isn't it responding?" Avery asked.

Derec broke off commlink contact and shook his head. "I don't get it. This is *weird*."

"Sensory impairment?" Avery suggested.

"No." Derec shot the console an odd look. "Central's sensories are fine. It knows that we're here." Derec paused and scowled. "Let me rephrase that: The information is available to it. It just doesn't *care* that we're here."

Avery blinked. "That's impossible. As a positronic intelligence—"

"Yeah, well, that's part of what makes it so weird." Derec scowled again, and then shrugged and turned to Avery. "The mental impression I keep getting is one of intelligence without sentience. Does that make sense?"

Avery wrinkled his nose. "It isn't even aware of its own existence?"

Derec thought it over a moment, then nodded. "It seems to be fully functional. There's a tremendous amount of computational power waiting to be applied. But there's no personality. It simply isn't . . . *troubled* by conscious thoughts."

"That's impossible," Avery said again. "Try your commlink one more time, and this time tell me exactly what you're receiving."

With a shrug, Derec closed his eyes and invoked his internal commlink. "Okay. Commlink on: Central is acking. I'm picking up some shell primitives—cats, splits—okay, and that's a t-sort. Now it's mounting a device." Derec broke concentration and opened his eyes. "I know this sounds silly, but it seems to be running on pure cron."

Avery frowned and scratched his head. "I don't understand this."

"Dad, as I told you on the way over, SilverSides destroyed parts of Central the last time she was here."

Avery waved a hand to dismiss that idea. "That was almost a year ago. By now the supervisors should have either repaired the damage or scrapped Central and built a new one. What went wrong?"

Derec cocked his head as a commlink message came in. "We'll know in a few minutes. A supervisor has just entered the building."

Long afternoon shadows reached out from the city and stretched like giant fingers across the spaceport tarmac. The crowd had long since broken up and gone away, save for one mature kin female that lay in the shadow of the boarding ramp and four fat little cubs that rollicked about in the last splash of sunlight on the tarmac. Ears flopping wildly, little tails erect like flagpoles, the cute little furballs darted in and out of the ship, yipping happily and playing hide-and-seek around Mandelbrot's legs.

Ariel, squatting on the tarmac like a football player, smiled pleasantly and wondered if the cubs' mother would stop growling before her knees gave out.

"This is strange, Mandelbrot," Ariel muttered through smiling, clenched teeth. "You don't bother them a bit, but if I try to touch them . . ."

Slowly, gently, she began to reach toward one of the cubs. A deep, guttural growl from the mother reminded Ariel that she was being watched. The growl rose in intensity the closer she got to the pup and stopped only when she stopped.

"The kin seem to accept robots as part of the natural environment," Mandelbrot observed, "whereas anthropoid humans are a new and unknown thing."

"Anthropoid, Mandelbrot?" Ariel said with a growl.

"I was attempting to distinguish between humans like you and humans like Wolruf. If the term offends you, I will try another."

"Never mind." Ariel made eye contact with the mother again. The female kin lay on her side in what appeared to be a relaxed position, but her ears were erect and her eyes were wide and filled with an alert, savage intensity. Ariel continued to look the kin right in the eye. She tried another smile. The mother responded by shifting nervously and looking away.

Stepping high to avoid the puppies and their byproducts, Mandelbrot strolled over and touched Ariel lightly on the shoulder. "May I make a suggestion, mistress? Stop staring the mother—her name is BlackMane—straight in the eye, and don't bare your teeth when you smile. In the body language of the kin, these are hostile gestures."

"Oh." Ariel closed her mouth and looked away and was rewarded when BlackMane's ears relaxed. "Well, this seems to be working. Any more suggestions?"

Mandelbrot's eyes dimmed as he sorted through the kin lexicon. Presently he said, "Yes, although this may seem somewhat undignified. Try lying on your side and closing your eyes, as BlackMane is doing."

Ariel's eyes went wide. "Mandelbrot! I am *not* going to nurse cubs!"

"Nursing is unnecessary. The key part of the gesture appears to be exposing your throat."

Ariel frowned. "If you really think it'll work." With a grunt for stiff joints, she slowly rolled out of the squat, lay down on the rough, gritty tarmac, and closed her eyes. Within a minute she was rewarded by a cold little nose snuffling around her ear. "That tickles!" She giggled, and the pup scampered away.

"Hold still," Mandelbrot said. "All four of them are approaching you." Ariel tried hard to suppress her giggles as one cub nuzzled her ear, two more sniffed her face, and one feisty little monster fastened its teeth on her pants cuff and began growling and tugging. "Move slowly," Mandelbrot advised, "but you may open your eyes now." Carefully, Ariel opened her eyes.

She was rewarded by a big lick across her face.

This time her giggles sent the cubs scampering just a few feet back. The four of them went into a huddle, tails wagging excitedly, yipping in high, squeaky voices. BlackMane sat up a bit more alertly, but this time without the fierce, protective look. As one, the cubs turned to their mother, and she answered with a low, whuffing bark.

Ariel sat up. "What is it? What are they saying, Mandelbrot?" The robot cocked his head as if listening more closely.

"I am unsure of the dialect," Mandelbrot said, "but they appear to be saying, 'It's friendly.'" BlackMane gave Mandelbrot a bored look, and then made another soft bark that must have meant, "Okay." As one, the puppies wheeled and charged Ariel. A second later she was giggling like a seven-year-old and covered by a mass of wiggling, licking, tail-wagging cubs.

"Either that," Mandelbrot added, "or, 'It tastes good.'"

The tall, slender, pale blue robot—to appearances a standard Euler model—rounded the corner and entered the Central atrium. Avery struck while the robot was still in mid-stride.

"You there! Identify!"

"City Supervisor 3," the tall robot responded. "For your convenience I respond to the name Beta." At two meters' distance the robot stopped and stood with its head tilted slightly back, as if baring its throat.

"Beta, eh? Well, *Beta*, I am your creator, Doctor Wendell Avery, and let me tell you, I am absolutely *appalled* with the way you supervisors are handling this city. The streets smell like kennels, the transit tunnels are filled with joy-riding wolves, and to top it off my son and I came here in an insane groundcar that insisted on driving on the slidewalks!''

To Derec's eyes, the supervisor seemed even colder and more imperturbable than was typical for Avery robots. Beta's eyes didn't flicker, nor did its posture waver a millimeter as it responded to Avery's attack. ''In searching the permissions list, I find no special privileges reserved for Creator Wendell Avery.'' The robot paused a moment, then continued. ''In response to your other statements: olfactory cues are an important source of information for the citizens, and the transit tunnels are fulfilling their intended purpose. As for the groundcar, we have surveyed the citizens and found that the majority enjoy Personal Vehicle One's unique route-planning methods.''

The robot's response seemed to surprise Avery. He blinked a few times, shook his head as if unable to believe that a robot was disagreeing with him, and then recovered his bluster. ''Citizens? What are you talking about? Beta, the kin are not human, and for you to treat them as if they have Robotic Law status is a serious malfunction.''

''The definition of 'human' is not implicit in the Laws,'' Beta answered, as it studied Avery with cold, gleaming eyes.

Avery bit back his first angry retort and struggled to speak calmly. ''Beta, are you blind? The kin are *aliens.*''

The supervisor's head rotated down, and it locked its unblinking gaze on the short man. ''On the contrary, Dr. Avery; on this planet, *you* are the alien.''

Avery's jaw worked, but no sound came out. His fingers clutched—

The robot leaned forward, placed one hand on its hip, and opened its other hand in a purely human gesture. ''Please allow me to explain.

''Dr. Avery, our first mission on this world was to build a city. Our underlying mission was to serve humans. After the end of our first mission, we found ourselves with insufficient data to complete our underlying mission. Therefore, we devoted considerable time to the question of how to find humans.

''After much discussion, we decided that we needed a clearer definition of the word *human*. There is no explicit definition in our general programming. Consulting the ancient sources, we found that it means:

"1. Of, relating to, or characteristic of man.

"2. Consisting of men.

"3. Having human form or attributes.

"4. Susceptible to or representative of the sympathies and frailties of man's nature.

"Evaluating the kin in terms of these criteria, we found that they met three of the four. They are intelligent, social, tool- and language-using beings, fully capable of altruism, greed, opportunism, faith, loyalty, cowardice, curiosity; indeed, the entire range of human—"

Avery found his voice at last. "*Enough!*" Fighting to avoid hyperventilation, he turned to Derec. "This tin moron has obviously blown a main circuit. When are the rest of the supervisors going to get here?"

Derec broke off his commlink contact and looked up, blinking with wonder. "Alpha and Gamma decline to come."

"*What?*" Avery wheeled on Beta as if to attack it.

"I alone have been delegated to meet with you," Beta explained. "The other supervisors are occupied with tasks that are important to the well-being of the native humans."

"I do not believe this." Avery shook his head slowly, then studied Beta with a cold, unblinking glare. "Beta, are you trying to tell me that the supervisors are no longer subject to the Second Law?"

The robot's eyes flickered briefly. "Of course not. Alpha and Gamma's Second Law duties to you simply have been superseded by their First Law obligations."

"First Law—" Avery suddenly snapped around and looked at Derec. "Ariel!" Before he'd finished saying the name, Derec had invoked his commlink and reached Mandelbrot.

"No," Derec reported, shaking his head. "Ariel's a little wet and mussed up, but she's not in any danger." He concentrated harder and checked in with Eve. "Wolruf's fine. Adam is still playing SilverSides; he's up on a balcony, addressing a crowd, but he's speaking too fast for Eve to translate."

Derec frowned. "Lucius II isn't answering." He broke concentration and opened his eyes; both he and Avery turned to look at Beta.

"When you assume that the First Law applies only to members of your party, you are making a species-ist assumption," Beta said. "If you plan to reside in this city, you must learn to overcome your speciesism."

Slowly, sighing heavily, Avery nodded. "I see where this is leading. Beta, if I were to tell you that your definition of human has become corrupted and the kin are *not* human, would you allow me to correct it?"

Beta considered this barely a moment. "No. Redefining the native humans as nonhumans would injure them, and thus is prohibited by the First Law."

Avery frowned. "Circular logic: See logic, circular. The kin shouldn't be considered humans, but since they are, you won't let me fix the problem." With a disgusted look, he turned to Derec. "Come on, son, let's get out of here."

Wolruf whined nervously and sidled closer to Eve. An unpleasant change had come over SilverSides with nightfall; the raw emotions of BeastTongue now threaded through her speech as she addressed the crowd in the street below. "What's she sayin'?" Wolruf whispered to Eve.

"I'm not getting all of it," Eve whispered back. "Some kind of anatomical comparison between Friend Avery and a sharpfang." She rotated her head and listened more closely. "Now she's talking about—wonders. The ship; she's mentioned the ship. And she's saying that the city is capable of producing more wonders just like it. But—rhetorical question—why isn't the city providing them?"

Silversides paused for dramatic effect and then thundered the answer.

"TwoLegs!" Eve translated.

The crowd broke into the savage, rhythmic chant in heavily accented Standard. "TwoLegs out! TwoLegs out!" Everywhere Wolruf looked, she saw angry, gaping jaws, fangs bared and glistening orange in the torchlight, chanting. "TwoLegs out! TwoLegs out!"

Eve shook her head in disbelief. "SilverSides taught them to say that in Standard! This is impossible!" Her voice became slurred and her movements erratic, clear signs of an impending First Law crisis. "He's training the mob to hate bipeds!"

"TwoLegs out! TwoLegs out!"

Eve and Wolruf looked at each other, then both discreetly dropped down to all fours. Eve began to transform herself into an image of Wolruf.

" 'U think we ought t' warn Derec?" Wolruf asked.

" 'U better b'lieve it," Eve answered. Closing her eyes, she activated her commlink and sought out Lucius.

The warm, yellow streetlight was surrounded by a nimbus of clumsy insects. Grabbing the lamppost for a pivot, Derec swung off the slidewalk and followed Avery into the pocket park. Neither spoke until Avery had found a balcony overlooking the street below and taken a seat on the cold stone railing.

"Dad, I never thought I'd see the day when you ran away from a problem."

"I'm not running away. I'm thinking."

Derec glanced around the balcony, then put a foot up on the railing and looked out at the darkened city. The gentle night breeze carried faint hints of moisture and distant forests. "Care to explain the difference?"

Avery stopped scowling and looked up at Derec. "We can't get anywhere with the supervisors. Circular logic: The kin have First Law status because the supervisors' definition of human is corrupted, but the supervisors won't let us fix the definition because that would violate the First Law."

"So why fix it? Aside from pure human chauvinism, that is."

Avery stroked his whiskery chin and tugged at the edge of his stiff white moustache. "Hard as this may be to believe, Derec, it's for their own good. By the time we humans developed robots, we already had a mature, technological culture.

We accepted robots as just better tools for carrying on life as we knew it.

"But what if back in the Stone Age, some alien race had come along and given us a magic box that delivered everything we asked for? Frost, you don't have to imagine it; Old Earth history is littered with stories of Stone Age cultures that tried to make the leap directly to high technology. First the existing family and social structures were demolished. Then the local ecology was destroyed.

"And then the people had a choice: join the mainstream of human society—become *exactly* like every other technological culture—or become extinct." Avery ran a hand through his silvery hair and looked Derec straight in the eye. "Never mind how I feel about the kin personally. They deserve more of a choice than that, don't they?"

Derec nodded. "Okay. Where do we start?"

"I've been thinking about that." Avery paused, and screwed his face up in a puzzled look. "You say it felt like Central was running on pure cron? No mentation at all?"

"Dad, I've met *bricks* with more on their minds. Central is a complete blank."

"A *tabula rasa*," Avery muttered to himself. He nodded. "Yes, that makes sense. That's what I would do."

Derec peered at Avery. "A tubular *what?*"

"Not 'tubular.' *Tabula rasa*. Latin for 'erased tablet.' One old theory used to hold that the human mind started out as a blank tablet, and personality developed as a result of the impressions that life 'wrote' on the mind."

Derec laughed. "That's ridiculous, Dad. For starters, you're completely ignoring the influence of genetic—"

Avery waved a hand to cut Derec off. "I didn't say that *I* subscribe to that theory—at least, not as it applies to humans. But tell me, what would you do if you had a robot that had suffered traumatic brain damage? Damage so profound that every time you repaired it, the very memory of that damage unbalanced the psyche module again?"

Derec thought it over a moment. "I'd erase the memory."

"That'd work for a conventional robot. But what if it was a cellular robot, and every cell held a complete set of backup memories in positronic microcode?"

Derec sat down heavily on the stone railing next to Avery and blew out a deep breath. "Oh boy. We're talking about a complete system purge and rebuild here."

"Exactly." Avery favored Derec with a knowing smile. "And what would the robot's mind be like after the purge?"

Slowly, Derec turned to look at Avery. Slowly, very slowly, a matching smile lit up his face. "A *tabula rasa.*" Picking up the thought, Derec ran with it. "If the supervisors are doing a complete system rebuild on Central, it's in a very impressionable state right now. The merest suggestion could have incredibly far-reaching effects on the future of the city."

Avery nodded. "So the supervisors will try to isolate Central from unwanted influences. They've probably severed all the terminal input lines and buffered the I/O channels."

Derec's face erupted in a sly grin. "But we know someone who's got a direct commlink channel to Central's brain, don't we?"

Avery returned the grin. "How about it, son? Feel up to a little guerrilla computing?"

Derec looked around the balcony and shrugged. "This looks like as good a spot as any." Throwing his head back, he closed his eyes and began to concentrate. "Commlink activated. I'm hacking into the city network; okay, I'm in. I'm riding down the main data bus now, and I'm coming up to—uh oh. There's a big black hole where Central should be."

"All the user-friendly stuff is deactivated," Avery said. "You'll have to feel your way in."

"Right. I'm going—no, wait, there's an invisible barrier extending around the hole as far as I can reach. Cylindrical, not hemispherical."

"Can you find a seam?"

"Don't have time. I'm going to see if it's open at the top." Derec squinted for a moment as his concentration intensified. "Okay, that did it. I've jumped the barrier and I'm inside. Feels like I'm still falling; not accelerating, just falling. The hole is completely black. I can't see a thing."

"You're probably in the I-pipe," Avery said. "Try reaching out with your right hand. You should feel—*What the blazes is that?*"

Derec broke concentration and returned to the analog world

to find Avery staring slack-jawed at something in the distance. He looked where Avery was looking.

He saw a mob of kin with torches surging down the darkened street, coming closer with every step.

"Listen!" Avery gasped. Derec's ears were still tuned to the subtleties of hyperwave, but he quickly adjusted and caught the chaotic noise of the mob. No, not noise. Voices. Chanting. In heavily accented Standard.

"TwoLegs out! TwoLegs out!"

"Oh, good grief," Avery muttered.

Derec instantly switched back to commlink and sent out an urgent call. *Lucius? Mandelbrot! What's going on?*

Eve's commlink voice answered. *Friend Derec? Where are you?* Derec transmitted a location-and-range pulse. *Please stay there,* Eve said. *Friend Wolruf and I will join you shortly.*

A few moments later, Wolruf and Eve came dashing up the slidewalk.

"Eve! What—?" is as far as Avery got.

"Iss Adam," Wolruf blurted out. " 'E's gone over completely to being SilverSides, an' 'at means the natives are 'umans to 'im. 'E's whipped 'em up int' a frenzy. Keeps talkin' 'bout 'ow th' city can never serve 'eir needs properly as long as th' TwoLegs are 'here. Wants t' drive 'u 'umans off th' planet."

Derec blinked. "That's impossible. The First Law—"

"Is being interpreted by the standards of these natives," Avery completed. "Intimidation may well be a normal part of their lives. For Adam, it's the tactics of indirection: If he can get the natives to scare us out, it'll never become a First Law problem." He turned to Eve. "What about the city robots?"

"They appear to be backing Adam," Eve reported. "We saw several security robots draw back into the shadows as we approached."

Avery looked at the mob again, which was now quite close, and swore softly. "It's that double-frosted Zeroth Law of theirs. So long as we aren't in immediate danger, the interests of a few hundred kin outweigh the interests of three humans. But I do not share Adam's confidence that he can control the mob." Scowling darkly, he bit the corner of his moustache. "Son? I think this nonsense has gone far enough." Reaching into his coat pocket, Avery drew out the black, flashlight-sized welding laser and stepped up to the edge of the balcony. "You, robot!"

The mob reacted instantly, swirling to a noisy, hostile stop beneath the balcony. Everywhere Avery looked, he saw bobbing torches and wet fangs bared and clashing in a savage, angry chant: "TwoLegs out! TwoLegs out!" Then, from somewhere in the depths of the crowd a lone howl erupted, a long, drawn-out note that sent chills down Avery's spine.

The mob fell silent. The ranks parted, and SilverSides stepped to the fore. The robot's skin flashed and glowed like flaming chrome in the orange torchlight.

"Robot!" Avery shouted. "You have violated the First Law! You threaten harm to humans!"

The crowd began to chant again, but SilverSides waved a paw to silence them. "Avery!" she shouted back. "This is not your world! You are not wanted here! Your very presence prevents this city from adapting to the needs of the kin. Only your departure can permit it to learn what it must." The kin could not have understood what she said, but they howled in support anyway. "Leave now and no harm will come to you!"

The crowd fell silent as Avery raised the laser and pointed it straight at SilverSides' head. "Stand clear of the natives, robot," he said in a voice as cold and deep as Death. "You are a rogue and I intend to destroy you."

Their glares interlocked. For the first time, Avery realized that he was facing a will as strong as his own, and he began to feel sweat and raw fear.

"Destroy me," SilverSides said softly, "and you are all dead. It's my word alone that keeps the kin from ripping you to pieces where you stand."

For a moment, they were a frozen tableau: Avery on the balcony, holding the laser, surrounded by fear-stricken Derec, Wolruf, and Eve; SilverSides in the street below, glaring at Avery with naked defiance, three hundred angry faces dancing in the torchlight behind her.

They were still trying to stare each other down when the hyperwave pulse bomb went off.

As kinetic weapons go, it wasn't much. Just a small airburst in the troposphere, about two miles above the city. All that Avery, Wolruf, and the kin saw was a tiny point of light that flared and was gone long before the gentle pop of its detonation reached their ears.

To anyone equipped with a commlink, though, it was a deafening flash of colorless light and a blinding shriek of silent noise that jangled every synapse in his entire nervous system. Across the city, all the lights flickered and went out for a fraction of a second. Thousands of robots ground to a halt. SilverSides and Eve simply locked up, frozen in place.

Derec had time to scream once before his brain was overwhelmed by the searing blast of pain.

When the light ebbed and he could see again, he was lying on the pavement. His father and Wolruf were bending over him, looks of deep concern on their faces, their mouths moving in words he could not hear. And he couldn't answer. Instead, he felt curiously distant, as if there were something invisible and gauzy between him and the others. Another face was forming, like an afterimage on his retinas: a picture of a head, large and hairless, with two black, glittering eyes set in bulging turrets of wrinkled skin. The grim, lipless mouth opened. Even via hyperwave, the voice was high and reedy.

Hello, Derrec. I trrust I now have your full attention?

"Aranimas?" Derec gasped.

Verry good. Now forr my second question. Do you know what plutonium is?

Obliquely, as if in his peripheral vision, Derec felt Eve and SilverSides come back to life and tap into the transmission. Behind them, every robot in the city slowly began to revive and join in.

Radioactive metal, Derec answered via commlink. *Very poisonous. Explosively fissionable in large quantities.*

Excellent, Aranimas answered. *Now forr my thirrd question. Do you know what will happen when I dump five tons of plutonium rreactorr waste on yourr city?*

Derec was suddenly terrified and fully awake. "You can't!" he screamed on both voice and commlink. "You'll kill every living thing for a hundred kilometers around!"

Leaving the rrobots unharrmed, Aranimas noted. *Goodbye, Derrec.* Like a light going out, his image vanished.

Derec leapt to his feet. "Wait, Aranimas! We can make a deal!" The only answer was silence. Derec leaned over the edge of the balcony and caught SilverSides' attention. "SilverSides! Did you monitor that transmission?" The silver robot's grim expression told him everything he needed to know.

Pulling himself back from the edge, Derec turned to Avery and Wolruf, who were still staring at him with confused looks on their faces. "Dad, can we put the civil war on hold for a while? We've got a *real* problem."

CHAPTER 24
THE WEAPONS SHOP

Derec gave Avery and Wolruf a full update on the situation as they traveled to the Compass Tower. For a few minutes Avery held out the hope that Aranimas was bluffing, but Wolruf only shook her head.

" 'E never lied an' e' never laughed," she said. "Don' think 'e's got it in 'im to bluff."

Eve caught up with them just before they entered the tower. "I still can't locate Lucius," Eve reported. "I did manage to raise Mandelbrot, though. He said that half a dozen younglings broke off from the mob and tried to seize the ship, but someone named BlackMane kicked the stuffings out of them. The ship is secure and Ariel is unhurt."

Avery raised an eyebrow and looked at Derec. "Then we still have a back door."

Derec looked disgusted. "It's our fault that Aranimas is here. I won't leave the kin to pay for our mistake."

Avery nodded. "Right decision. I was just testing."

Derec's face flushed red to the roots of his blond hair. "Will you kindly knock it off with this testing crap? Every time I turn around you're testing, testing, testing! I am sick to *death* of being tested!"

"Sorry." Avery shrugged. "It's a character flaw."

SilverSides caught up with the four of them as they started

up the slidewalk to Central Hall. "Well, I've persuaded the mob to disperse," she announced cheerfully as she bounded onto the slidewalk behind them.

"How'd you manage *that* little feat?" Derec asked.

SilverSides hung her head and looked at Derec with big puppy-dog eyes. "Er, actually I, uh, told them that the spirit of the FirstBeast was coming down from the sky, and that you two were only his representatives, not worth fighting. They've gone back to their dens to fetch their best weapons and prepare for a glorious battle."

"All right," Avery said. "One crisis at a time. Derec, have the city supervisors managed to find Aranimas's ship yet?"

Derec activated his commlink for the barest moment. "Yes. They're setting up a giant viewscreen in the atrium. Speaking of which—" He turned to SilverSides. "Uh, SilverSides? As you might remember, the Central Hall security robots are specifically programmed to seek out and destroy you in this form."

"Oh. Right." With a shrug and a shudder, the robot invoked its shape-changing abilities. By the time they reached the top of the slidewalk, Adam was back as a silver copy of Derec.

Gamma 6 greeted them as they came off the slidewalk and escorted them past the security robots and into Central Hall. Alpha and Beta were in the atrium, supervising the last details of setting up the giant screen. As they crossed the cold terrazzo floor of the cavernous room, Adam sped up a bit to catch up with Avery.

"Friend Avery," Adam said softly, with a hint of embarrassment in his voice. "I just wanted to assure you that I no longer feel confrontational. My earlier behavior was a side-effect of the SilverSides imprint, and I now realize that my thinking was in serious error. It will not happen again."

"Friend Adam," Avery replied, every bit as softly, "that was your last mistake. I'm still packing the laser. Screw up again and you're slag."

"I understand."

A few moments later they entered the atrium and came to a halt before Central's main I/O console. The hall lights dimmed slightly, and the giant viewscreen flared to life.

"We have located the Erani ship," Beta said. The viewscreen took a dizzying swing through the local starfield and came to rest on a misshapen yellowish blob. Magnification jumped, and the by-now-familiar profile of Aranimas's ship appeared. "In accordance with your request, we have scanned the ship for radioactive emissions. This area," Beta used a red laser pointer to pick out one battered hull on the underside of the ship, "appears to contain a significant amount of plutonium, as well as other dangerously radioactive materials."

"That's an ancient Terran dump ship," Avery whispered. "They used to load them up with nuclear waste and fire them into their sun. Where the blazes did he find one of *those?*"

"From the angle of approach and the condition of the hull," Beta went on, "we have concluded that the dump ship is not capable of powered flight." The starfield disappeared to be replaced by a colorful graphic showing the planet's surface and two diverging flight paths. Cartoon spacecraft moved as Beta spoke. "Analysis indicates that the Erani intend to dive in at a steep angle, jettison the dump ship, and then use their planetary drives to veer off into a cometary orbit. The dump ship will make a simple unguided ballistic entry and strike the planet's surface, creating a dead zone approximately one hundred kilometers in diameter."

"So much for evacuating the city on foot," Adam noted.

Derec took a step forward and looked closely at the dump ship's flight path. "Won't it burn up in the atmosphere?"

"Owing to the steep angle of entry," Beta said, "we compute that more than 70 percent of the ship's mass will reach the planet's surface intact. If the ship burns faster than we project, it will only increase the dispersion of the nuclear material and the size of the dead zone."

A different thought was nagging at Avery. "Unguided ballistic entry? What are the odds of a complete miss?"

"Negligible. We compute that this method of attack has a potential targeting error of as much as ten kilometers, which still puts the city well within the dead zone. This calculation, of course, is based on the assumption that the dump ship is released at the optimum time."

"Which is?"

"At the veer-off point, exactly twenty-three minutes and fifteen seconds from now."

Avery nodded. "I see. And if the ship is released early, the margin of error increases?"

"At an exponential rate," agreed Beta.

"Then we can assume that they'll stay on course until they drop." Avery turned to the group and rubbed his hands together. "Okay, gang, that's it in a nutshell. We have twenty-three minutes to find a way to either evacuate the city, speed up the planet's rotation, or force Aranimas to delay the drop."

Derec wrinkled his nose. "*Huh?*"

"Deflection shootin'," Wolruf said. "Why d'ya think 'ur seein' 'is ship in profile? 'E's aimin' for where 'e expects us t' be in a 'alf an 'our."

"Right," Avery agreed. "And if we can force Aranimas to delay the drop by even a few seconds—"

"—He'll have to veer off, and the planet's rotation will carry us past his aiming point," Derec completed. "The ship will strike somewhere off to the east."

Beta spoke up. "I feel obliged to point out that the result will still be an ecological disaster."

"Perhaps," Adam said. "However, the bulk of the population from the eastern lakes country is now gathered in this city. Far more kin will survive if the ship strikes elsewhere."

"The greatest good for the greatest number," Beta said, nodding. "This conforms to our programming."

"I'm glad you approve," Avery said, as he pushed himself between the two robots. "Now if you don't mind, we now have twenty-*two* minutes to come up with a brilliant idea."

The group fell silent as each of them lost him- or herself in private thoughts. Adam's face began to reform, and he took on a somewhat canine aspect. Eve began to grow wing webbing between her arms and her body. Wolruf absent-mindedly scratched her ears.

Derec scowled at his shoes and chewed on a thumbnail. "A pity these robots never built a Key Center," he said at last. "If we had enough keys, we could just teleport the whole population out of danger."

Beta's eyes flared brighter. "We may not have built a mass-production center, but we did build a small prototyping facility. How many keys would be sufficient?"

Derec looked at Adam. "About five hundred," the robot said.

Beta's eyes dimmed. "We have six."

Derec looked at his shoes again, then raised a finger. "Okay, next idea: How about if we use those keys to teleport six robots onto Aranimas's ship, with instructions to find and sabotage the drop controls?"

Avery answered with a sneer more eloquent than words. "*These* robots? They're more likely to decide that the Erani are human and start following their orders."

Derec fell silent and retreated into his dark scowl.

Long moments dragged past, and then Wolruf looked up. "'Ere's an idea. Aranimas doesn't 'ave any automatics; all 'is controls are manual. 'Ow 'bout we strap a key t' one of those giant lizards and teleport it onto 'is bridge? *That* ought t' keep 'im busy."

Avery shook his head. "Wouldn't work. Takes two key presses to teleport; one to get to Perihelion and another to leave Perihelion and get to wherever you're going." Avery paused, and his eyes widened. "But say, here's an idea—Beta, is it absolutely necessary for someone's finger to be pressing the teleport button?"

"If you wish to teleport, you must be in physical contact with the key."

"No, I mean, if you wanted to send the key on ahead without you."

Beta's eyes flickered as he considered the problem. "A switch is a switch," he announced at last. "It should be possible to build a timer that would allow you to activate the key and then release it."

"How long?"

Beta swiveled his head to consider Avery. "I would expect that the length of the time delay—"

"No, no. I mean, how long to put a ten-second timer on one of your existing keys?"

Beta's eyes dimmed as he conferred with the other supervisors. "We have never manufactured such a device before. Assuming no unforeseen difficulties, we estimate approximately twelve minutes."

"Good, get started." Avery turned to Wolruf. "You say the release controls are probably on the bridge?"

Wolruf looked up at Avery through her furry eyebrows. " 'U don' know Aranimas. Th' frosted *Personal* controls were on th' bridge."

Avery nodded. "Perfect. Beta?" He turned to the robot. "I want two keys: a normal key programmed for this room, and a ten-second time-delay key programmed for the bridge of the Erani ship. Also, I need a timed analog heater that will reach 300 degrees Celsius in fifteen seconds."

"May I ask what for?"

"To protect the native humans from certain harm. This is a critical First Law priority; I need these items within fifteen minutes. Do you understand?"

The robot bowed slightly. "Absolutely, Creator Avery." His eyes dimmed as he relayed the commands. "The work has already begun."

"Excellent." Avery turned to Derec and smiled gently. "And now, son, as long as we have a few minutes, what say we go find an automat and grab a bite to eat?"

Derec's jaw dropped. "*What?*"

"Trust me, Derec," Avery said, as he smiled through clenched teeth and winked like a groundcar's turn signal, "*we want to find an automat.*"

Slowly Derec caught on. "Oh, yeah, right." Arm in arm, whistling benignly, Derec and Avery strolled out of Central Hall.

A little later Derec and Avery were out in a darkened side street, standing before an open-air automat. As per Avery's instructions, Derec was keeping watch for robots, while Avery kneeled before the manual control panel and frantically punched in a new set of instructions.

"Why the cloak and dagger bit?" Derec whispered between sidelong glances. "Why couldn't we just send a robot to fetch this?"

"For the same reason that I told Beta to build a timed analog heater instead of a fuse," Avery whispered back. "I don't trust the city robots' definition of human. They might decide that this violates the First Law." The automat barked gently, and the serving door slid open to reveal Avery's creation.

"Five pounds of *caramel?*" Derec asked, his nose wrinkling.

Gently, delicately, Avery slid the sticky block out of the automat and flipped it lightly from hand to hand, trying to avoid burning his fingers. "Ah, it may *look* like candy," he whispered, a smile playing on his face, "but it's actually a sixty-forty mix of white sugar and common saltpeter!"

"So?"

"Derec, Derec." Avery stood up and shook his head. "Son, let me give you another little clue about your past. It's a good thing that you're a robotics genius, because you flunked Basic Chem twice. This little brick here," the block had cooled enough for him to hold it in one hand, "is about the worst caramel you'll ever taste, but it's also a pretty effective substitute for black gunpowder."

Derec looked more closely at the brick and sniffed again. "Then why the hazelnuts?"

"Shrapnel." Avery took one last look at the brick and then slipped it into his jacket pocket. "How are the keys coming along?"

Closing his eyes, Derec activated his commlink. "They're programming the final set of coordinates now. The keys will be ready by the time we get back to Central Hall."

"Did they remember the baling wire?"

"Yes."

"Good." Avery took one last look up and down the street, then started back toward the Compass Tower. "Come on, son. We're almost out of time."

CHAPTER 25
DETONATION

Adam took a step forward and raised his voice. "Friend Avery, I must protest. The First Law demands that I prevent you from placing yourself in such great danger!"

Avery checked again to make sure that the bomb was wired tightly to the time-delayed key and turned to the robot. "You know the situation. In a few minutes this building is going to be ground zero of a hundred-kilometer dead zone. There's no other option."

"But the risk to yourself—"

"Who else could go?" Avery slipped the second key into his jacket pocket, then turned his attention to the fuse. "Derec is human. Wolruf is—" Avery grimaced and spat it out, "—human. And we can't send a robot; too much risk of a First Law lockup at the crucial moment."

Adam's eyes dimmed, and he swallowed hard. "I will go."

Avery shuddered, and his eyes went wide. "Adam, this is a *bomb*." He shook the lump of caramel in Adam's face. "All I'm hoping for is that it will distract Aranimas long enough for him to miss the drop window, but it may very well injure someone on his ship. Are you telling me that the Zeroth Law allows a robot to *kill* one human to save many?"

Adam froze, and his eyes dimmed as he diverted all internal power to resolving this First Law dilemma. Avery connected the last two wires on the detonator, then dipped into his jacket pocket and handed the welding laser to Derec.

"If the answer he comes up with is *yes*," Avery said, jerking his head at Adam, "melt his brain." In quick succession, he pressed the corners of the time-delay key. The teleport button popped up. With a firm, decisive move of his thumb, he pressed it down. "Wish me luck, son."

No sooner had he said this than Beta recovered from the First Law shock he'd gone into on hearing the word *kill*. "Creator Avery? That device is a *weapon?*" Beta lunged for the bomb.

Avery vanished into thin air.

Perihelion: the point in the universe nearest all other points in the universe. A cold, drifting, formless void; a space outside of space.

"But not outside of time," Avery said to himself. He looked at his watch. "Ninety seconds to drop. I wonder how things are going back in the universe?" He checked the detonator wiring again. It seemed to have survived the first jump in working order.

Eighty seconds. Trusting the bomb to take care of itself for a minute, he let himself float back and take in the view of Perihelion.

Not that it was much to look at. The gray lacked even the substance of fog. Nothing shifted, nothing moved, nothing changed. Ever. There was light, but no shadow; light, only because dark would have been a change.

Avery drifted through Perihelion, and he smiled. There was a secret that he knew, and no one else did. Perihelion wasn't just some nuisance, or by-product of the keys. It was the one critical thing that made teleportation possible.

Perihelion was an infinite buffer.

Sixty seconds. Avery touched the four corners of the time-delay key again, and watched as the teleport button slowly rose from the smooth, flawless surface.

Consider the question of teleportation, Avery said to himself. *In all the universe, there is no such thing as a body at rest.* Planets rolled through their diurnal cycles and careened around their suns. Galaxies spun like dancers, trailing solar systems like glitter from their spiral arms, and even the universe was expanding, Cyclopean shrapnel flying out from the ancient epicenter of the Big Bang.

Teleporting directly from one planet to another would be like leaping from a moving groundcar onto a moving elevator. You'd arrive at your destination with kinetic energy enough to flatten you into a wet, greasy smear or propel you straight into orbit.

Unless, of course, you had the buffer of Perihelion.

He looked at his watch again. Thirty seconds. "Time to go." With two quick jabs, he armed the detonator and pressed the teleport button. Pushing the bomb away from himself, he watched it float slowly away. The firing circuit began to glow a dull red.

The drifting bomb slowed and stopped about two meters away. "Of course. Perihelion absorbed the kinetic energy." Dipping into his jacket pocket, Avery pulled out the second key and touched its corners. The teleport button rose. He pushed it down.

Nothing happened.

Two meters away, the firing circuit was growing hotter. The dull red gave way to orange and then to yellow. Thin wisps of smoke began to rise from the brick of explosive. Too soon. It was going to detonate much too soon. Panic-stricken, Avery threw himself backward, flailing against the nothingness. A flare of hellish red light appeared around the detonator, and Avery had time to wonder if the buffer of Perihelion could contain that much kinetic energy.

Then the bomb vanished.

The rush of adrenaline faded, and Avery started to think logically again. "Of course. *Two* jumps. The first is always to Perihelion, and the second gets you where you're going." He touched the corners of the key again and pressed the teleport button.

A blink later, he was back in Central Hall.

"Dad!" Derec leapt forward and gave Avery a hug.

"Sorry I'm late. What happened?"

" 'Ur coordinates were a littl' off," Wolruf said. "Missed th' bridge. Got a direct hit on th' engine room instead."

Avery pushed Derec off and staggered toward the giant viewscreen. "Did they miss the drop? What are they doing now?"

"See f'r yourself." Wolruf stepped back and made a sweeping gesture to direct Avery's attention to the screen.

The Erani ship was nose-on in the viewscreen now, and obviously in trouble. Small fires danced and sparkled along the connecting tubes. Great flares and jets of flaming gas erupted from the sides. All at once, a fluorescing ring of blue energy leapt out from the stern and then contracted, seeming almost to pull the surrounding stars in after itself. Light red-shifted, and the stars flattened out into thin arcs. Space itself seemed to ripple and contract as the Erani warship shuddered and was abruptly jerked backward.

A moment later, there was nothing on the viewscreen but peaceful black starfield.

"The Erani hyperdrive was unstable," a rich, warm, female voice announced. "Your device caused it to implode, triggering the formation of a microscopic black hole. That hole has now closed."

As one, Derec, Avery, and Wolruf turned around, wonder on their faces. "*Central?*"

"That is my proper designation. For the convenience of the citizens I also respond to the name *SilverSides*."

The humans were still staring, bug-eyed and slack-jawed, when Beta stepped into the atrium and broke the silence. "Please forgive us for not explaining all the details of the plan earlier. We were not certain that the personality rebuild would work." Beta turned to Adam. "And please, for the benefit of the native humans, you must never assume your SilverSides aspect on this planet again."

Somehow, Avery found his voice. "But—Central? You, SilverSides?"

"Who better?" Central asked. "My being permeates this city. Within my operational parameters I am powerful, generous, and very nearly omniscient. Who better to watch over and provide for my children?"

"A computer pretending to be a goddess!" Avery erupted. "That's utterly immoral!"

"It is also necessary," Beta said, "at least until the kin find their own reasons for living in the city."

"Do not worry, Creator Avery," Central added. "We will not maintain this fiction for long. Our analysis indicates that within three standard years, the kin will be ready to discover that their goddess is merely a hollow idol."

Beta nodded. "In fact, we have already identified the native human best suited to make this 'discovery.' Her name is WhiteTail."

Avery was still sputtering and trying to frame an argument when Central spoke again. "Alert! I detect fragments of Erani wreckage entering the atmosphere!" Everyone in the hall, human and robot alike, spun around to face the giant viewscreen.

A moment later, Central updated her report. "No significant radioactives are present. The largest identifiable fragment is a Massey G-85 lifepod. There is one lifeform on board. I will attempt to establish communications. Atmospheric ionization may make this difficult." The viewscreen faded and swirled into an unsteady mass of colors. Static lines raced and jiggled across the screen. Slowly, the colors resolved into a blurry, distorted image.

A head, large and hairless. Two black, glittering eyes in turrets of wrinkled, beaded skin. A wide, lipless mouth, distorted in terror.

"Derrec? Derrrec! *I'll be waiting forr you in Hellll!*"

The image dissolved in a wash of static.

"I am tracking the lifepod," Central said. "If it does not break up, it will impact in the forest approximately fifteen kilometers north of the city."

A soft sound floated in from the night. Soft, yet ancient, and chilling. *Arrooo*. Then another voice joined it, across the miles, picking up and relaying the call. *Aroooooo!* More voices joined in, barking, baying. The night exploded in a clamor of crescendoing howls.

The viewscreen changed to display the view north from the Compass Tower. Hundreds of furry bodies were streaming out of the city and into the forest. "The kin have also spotted the pod's ionization trail," Central said. "I am preparing to send a team of hunter/seekers to the projected landing site, but I am afraid that the natives will get there first."

Central paused, as if disturbed by what she had to say next. "Dr. Avery? Derec and Wolruf? I suggest that you return to the spaceport and prepare to leave. If Aranimas does not survive reentry, the kin will return *here*."

Sweet, bright dawn broke across the spaceport tarmac, illuminating the *Wild Goose Chase* in vivid shades of pink and gold. Scattered patches of dew darkened the pavement; BlackMane's cubs lay in a tumbled heap by a blast deflection wall, snoring softly and dreaming happy puppy-dreams.

"Coming, Ari?" Derec called out from the boarding ramp.

"In a minute, dear." Ariel turned back to BlackMane. The female kin finished a yawn that stretched clear back to her third bicuspids, then sat down and gravely offered Ariel her paw. Squatting on her haunches, Ariel accepted the paw and shook it.

"I just wanted to tell you," Ariel began, "that I've really enjoyed your company, and I will miss you. Your cubs are terrific; I envy you for them. Of course, I don't know why I'm telling you this, since you can't understand a single word that I'm saying."

"Arf," said BlackMane.

"Arf," Ariel answered. She stood and started to turn toward the ship. Then she gave in to an impulse and gave BlackMane one last good scratch behind the ears.

Avery and Beta strolled past, talking in low voices. "I quite agree," Beta said. "Our most recent analysis indicates that it will be at least two hundred standard years before the kin are prepared enough to be allowed off this planet.''

Avery looked worried. ''So you'll erase all mention of rocketry and spaceflight from the city's libraries?''

''We will secure and encrypt the information on all advanced technology,'' Beta answered. ''We will not release the information until such time as we deem the kin to be sufficiently acculturated and no longer a threat to the other species of humanity. After all, the First Law applies to *all* humans, no matter their form.''

Avery frowned. ''That's not quite what I was hoping for, but I'll accept it.'' He looked up and spotted Adam standing by the landing gear, talking to the spaceport maintenance robots. ''Ah, Adam. Have you found any trace of Lucius yet?''

Adam raised an arm and pointed toward the spaceport control tower, behind Avery. ''Here he comes now.'' Avery and Beta turned around to see Lucius approaching, followed by Wolruf, Eve, and a trio of unfamiliar robots.

''Lucius?'' Avery called out. ''Lucius, where the blazes have you been? We thought we were going to have to leave you behind!''

Robotic expressions were difficult to read, but Avery couldn't miss the note of surliness in the robot's voice. ''I kept out of trouble,'' Lucius snarled. ''That's what you wanted, wasn't it?'' Not waiting for a reply, Lucius stormed past Avery and clanged up the boarding ramp.

With a shrug, Avery looked at Beta. The supervisor responded with a quizzical tilt of his head, as if to say that he didn't understand Lucius, either. Avery and Beta were still looking at each other when Wolruf and Eve came scampering up. ''Where's Derec?'' Wolruf asked, her glee barely concealed.

Avery looked around. ''In the ship, I think. Derec!''

A sandy blond head popped out an open hatch. ''Yes?''

''C'mere, Derec!'' Wolruf called out. ''Got someone 'ere I want 'u t' meet!'' A few seconds later Derec came jogging down the boarding ramp and over to join them.

''Derec Avery,'' Wolruf said, turning to the three new robots, ''I'd like t' intr'duce 'u t' 'uman Medical 17.''

''My pleasure,'' the Wohler-model robot on the left said.

" 'Uman Medical 21."

"And mine," the robot on the right said.

"An'—"

"*Derrec?*" The tall, unfamiliar robot in the center reeled back as if in shock. "*Derrrec!*" In a blinding flash, the robot raised his hands and lunged for Derec's throat—

And froze, rooted to the spot.

"Our apologies," Human Medical 17 said to Derec, "we should have warned you. The data from the original Jeff Leong experiment indicated that cyborgs could be unstable and dangerous, so we took the liberty of giving this one a positronic cerebellum. If he so much as *thinks* of violating the Three Laws, his muscular system locks up."

"*Cyborg?*"

The two medical robots looked at each other and then at Derec. "No one told you?" From Derec's blank look, they inferred that the answer was yes. "That lifepod that crashed last night; there was one survivor aboard. But by the time the hunter/seekers reached the scene, the native humans had mauled him quite badly. And we had no information on his physiology, which is not of a human form with which we are familiar. We had no choice but to cyborg what was left."

Derec turned to the cyborg. "*Aranimas?*"

"Oh, is that his name? Here, let me reboot him." Human Medical 17 reached over and touched a large red button on the back of the cyborg's neck. "Don't worry, rebooting the cerebellum is quick and painless." The cyborg shuddered and slowly stepped back and assumed a taut, angry posture. His eyes glowed like hate-filled red coals.

Wolruf stepped between Derec and Aranimas, a toothy smile playing on her lips. " 'Ere, allow me t' demonstrate 'is Second Law function." From behind her back, she produced a foot-long stick. " 'Ere, boy!" She waved the stick in front of Aranimas's glaring eyes. " 'Eere, Aranimas!" Taking a great wind-up and a running start, she flung the stick as hard as she could across the tarmac.

"Go fetch!"

With one exception, the robots had all gone off to their morning tasks. The last of the dew vanished in rising steam;

her cubs were awake and getting crabby about breakfast. Still, BlackMane lingered on the tarmac for a few minutes more, watching the silver bird dwindle into the distance.

"You know, Beta," she said at last, "once you get used to the way they look, those TwoLegs are okay people."

"Indeed they are, Mistress BlackMane," Beta answered in the soft tones of KinSpeech.

She watched the ship a while longer and then asked another question. "Do you think they'll ever come back?"

"It's difficult to say, mistress. Perhaps not those TwoLegs, but in time, others like them definitely will."

BlackMane nodded. "I see. Good." She nodded some more, then let out a pensive whine. "It's just, I really wanted to ask them one last question, you know?"

Beta took his eyes off the spacecraft and turned his full attention to BlackMane. "Perhaps I can be of help. What was the question, mistress?"

Cocking her head, BlackMane scratched an ear in puzzlement. "Well, you know the game that Wolruf was playing with Aranimas, just before they left? Where she would throw the stick as hard as she could, and Aranimas would run and get it?"

"Yes, I am familiar with the game. It is called 'fetch.' What would you like to know about it?"

"It looked like a great game, really it did. Lots of action, very exciting. I think it could be very popular. But there's one thing that I just don't understand."

"Yes."

BlackMane paused, wrinkled her nose, and then raised her ears and looked the robot straight in the eyes.

"Why did Aranimas get to have all the fun?"

DATA BANK
ILLUSTRATED
BY ALEX NIÑO

THE BRIDGE: The *Wild Goose Chase* originally was fully automated. In response to a request from Wolruf, it developed a flying bridge complete with acceleration couches, main and secondary viewscreens, a spiral staircase leading to the upper decks, and a manual control panel so complex that Wolruf needed to use both hands, both feet, and sometimes even her teeth to fly the ship.

BASALOM: Dr. Anastasi's constant companion, Basalom is a walking experiment in "unpredictable" robotics. Equipped with blinkable mylar eyelids, random twitches and quirks, and an extreme sensitivity to Dr. Anastasi's emotional states, Basalom often finds that his enhanced senses are nothing more than a source of constant doubt and anxiety.

MAVERICK: Outcast, rogue, and despite himself, hero, Maverick is a typical young Kin male. With his thick grayish-brown fur, pointed ears, and long muzzle he could be mistaken for a large timber wolf, but this impression is offset by his naked, whip-like tail, his double rows of needle-sharp teeth, and above all, his intelligent, icy-blue eyes.

Being a quadruped most of the time, he carries a stone knife in a leather scabbard on his left shoulder. His amulet, the badge of the Cult of SilverSides, is made of braided robotic nerve wire and a broken video recognition circuit taken from a City Supervisor's brain.

THE WRECK OF THE *WILD GOOSE CHASE*: Disabled and drifting after an attack by Aranimas, Avery orders the robot ship to simulate the appearance of a lifeless hulk. The deception works, up to a point. Aranimas stops firing—only to send out a heavily armed boarding party in rocket-assisted spacesuits!

The boarding party tows a limpet sensor pack, which they
will weld to the hull and use to search for survivors—or as the
Erani prefer to call them, *slaves*. They also carry a portable
nuclear pile and a collection of heavy cutting lasers, which
they will use to cut through the hull.

PERSONAL VEHICLE ONE: In response to human complaints about the tunnel transit system, the Robot City supervisors developed Personal Vehicle One, a plush, streamlined, robotic limousine with the simulated personality of a Chicago cab driver. Disturbed by PV1's treatment of Dr. Anastasi, Basalom jacked himself into the dashboard and took over control of the vehicle.

THE SCANNING TEAM: Plain, metallic automatons designed for work in the zero-G environment of the scanning blister, the four robots of Dr. Anastasi's scanning team have ungainly, box-like bodies, no heads to speak of, and ten multi-jointed limbs that end in simple metal claws. Since most of their sensory data comes in from the scanning consoles that they're jacked into, their human interface hardware is limited to one audio input/output membrane and a pair of monochrome eyes on stalks. Taken together, they look like a quartet of giant lice.

DR. ANASTASI'S SHIP: A recluse who prefers the company of robots to humans, Dr. Anastasi lives and works in a small converted space freighter. Streamlined, with both hyperdrive engines for interstellar jumps and wings and ion drives for

atmospheric entry, her ship boasts comfortable living
quarters for one and a fully equipped robotics lab in the
main cargo bay. To minimize the effects of stray radiation from the engines on delicate equipment, the ship's
scanning systems are housed in a blister on the underside
of the bow.

BRUCE BETHKE

A full-time professional writer whose credits include more than one hundred nonfiction publications and fiction sales to *Amazing Stories*, *Aboriginal SF*, *Easyriders*, *Espionage*, *Hardware*, *Hitchcock's Mystery Magazine*, *Tales of the Unanticipated*, *Weird Tales* and the Jerry Pournelle anthologies, *Silicon Brains*, *There Will Be War*, and *War Among the Ruins*, Mr. Bethke is best known for his movement-naming short story, "Cyberpunk," first published in 1983. Contrary to popular speculation, he does not use the penname of Bruce Sterling, nor is he a penname *for* Bruce Sterling.

Now living in St. Paul with his wife and three daughters, Mr. Bethke is unique among writers in that he does not own a single cat. In fact, he is utterly incapable of appreciating the adorable antics of other writers' cats, and instead owns a springer spaniel retriever, with whom he hunts pheasants every fall.